Frozen in Time

Sandy Brannan

This book is dedicated to Carie and Rhonda for your unrelenting support of my writing.

Sandy Brannan

ISBN: 9798565128703

Prologue

May 17, 2015

"We've been so blessed." Pausing to catch his breath as he struggled to lift up a bit off the hospital bed, Robert stared at his wife as he continued, "Babe, you'll always have me with you, but you need to know we aren't going to be together much longer."

Watching her husband's face as he easily admitted what she refused to accept, Kayleigh forced herself to not look away. She didn't have the luxury of time or of denying what was right in front of her. Taking in every detail, she knew the way he looked at this moment would forever be etched in her mind. His green eyes, once full of laughter, were now dull with pain. She noticed he needed a shave, then forced back a sob as she realized she would never see him lather his face up again at the bathroom sink they had shared on too many mornings to count. His lips, although swollen and beginning to bruise, still called to her. Reaching down to him, Kayleigh let her mouth softly graze over his. She couldn't bear the thought of causing him pain, but she also knew she shouldn't pass up this last chance to kiss her husband, this man who was her world.

Robert's voice was raspy and labored as he added, "Our love transcends time. I'll never stop loving you, no matter what." Hearing his final words almost broke her heart. Twenty-five years together felt like no time at all. She felt like they had just started living their life, and now, because of a stupid accident, it was suddenly over. Watching his eyes flutter shut, she held him even closer. She wanted to soak in his warmth, to feel his body next to hers. Fighting back tears, she keenly felt what was missing, arms that weren't around her where they belonged. Knowing he was already gone, she gave in to the need to cling to what was left of him, if only for a little while. It frightened her to know that once she let go, once she walked out of this hospital room, she would truly be alone. The thought shook her to her core.

When the hospital had called her earlier, it had taken several seconds to understand what was going on. She heard words that made sense separately, but when put together her brain refused to comprehend their meaning. She made out her husband's name and the words accident and hospital before she jumped up from her desk, barely remembering to grab her purse and car keys. With a silent sob holding her voice hostage, there wasn't time to explain to anyone why she was leaving.

Heading toward the hospital mere minutes later, closer to Robert with every mile that passed, she prayed like she never had before. She couldn't stop the tightness that was squeezing her chest. When she finally pulled into the parking lot, she had to sit there, wasting precious seconds, just to get her heartrate under control. Getting out of the car, she ran toward the doors of the emergency department. Out of breath when she reached the person at admissions, she cringed when she heard her voice squeak out her husband's name. Had she imagined the look that crossed the lady's face before she called someone to escort her to the room where Robert was?

When the nurse pulled the curtain back, Kayleigh dropped her purse to the floor, not caring that half of its contents rolled out. She only focused on the sad eyes staring back at her from the hospital bed, her own unable to see anything else. She didn't need a doctor to tell her that her husband's body was broken beyond repair. Putting her face as close to his as possible, she failed to control her sobs as she told him of her love. Tears made their way down his cheeks as he spoke his final words meant only for her before closing his eyes for the last time.

A startling sound from one of the machines hooked up to her husband had made her grab his shoulders and shake him, begging him to please look at her again. When the nurse gently pulled her away, Kayleigh didn't put up a fight. When she was taken to a room with only a couch and a chair, she sat down shakily and stared at the wall. When her best friend appeared at her side sometime later, she finally looked up. Finally admitted this was all real.

Kayleigh would never remember what happened those next few hours. Somehow she got home and was put into her bed, the one she had shared with the love of her life for the past two decades. Later she would learn about the sedative her doctor had prescribed. Later she would be told who went back to pick up her purse and her car. Later she would find out who had made the funeral arrangements for her husband. She would never remember any of it.

But the image of seeing Robert in that hospital bed would forever be etched in her mind, frozen in time.

Chapter One

Summer 2015

Kayleigh sighed as she reached her desk, pausing to hang her purse on the decorative peg put there years ago for just that purpose. Looking at it for a few seconds too long, she couldn't help but remember the day Robert had shown up at her office with a huge smile on his face, a hammer in the back pocket of his jeans, and a tiny bag in his hand. Apparently she had shared one time too many how her purse constantly got in her way at work and he had decided he could fix this problem for her. She allowed herself to smile as she remembered how she had whispered in his ear that he was her knight in shining armor while hugging him before he left her office that day. He had only looked at her in that gentle way he had, but it had been enough to let her know how he was feeling. She knew giving her a place to hang her purse wouldn't be a big deal to most people, but to her it had meant everything.

Shaking her head to move the ever-present memories out

of the way, Kayleigh turned toward her desk, glancing down at the calendar before sitting in her swivel chair. She refused to follow the memory trail again. Yes, Robert had given her this chair as an anniversary present, but she had work to do. She couldn't continue to spend all her time in the past with her husband, her dead husband. Flinching as that awful word came to her mind, she let her eyes linger on the last picture she had taken of him. He had been outside playing basketball when she had, on impulse, pulled out her phone to take a quick snapshot. She had planned to show it to him later and tease him about how he still had the same moves he had been famous for in college, but she had never gotten the chance. She had forgotten about the picture until she stumbled upon it after the funeral. Now she was grateful to have it. Looking at his image helped keep him alive for her, at least for the few seconds she allowed herself to stare at it every day.

Turning on her computer helped her focus on the work ahead of her. She still needed the mental pep talk she gave herself daily to get through her eight hours of work. Nothing distracted her anymore, breaking up the monotony of her job. There certainly weren't random texts arriving throughout the day. Texts that had always made her smile, always made her grateful for the man she had married. No, her phone was silent now. In fact, she really didn't even need it anymore if she were being honest with herself, but she couldn't seem to find the energy to cancel her plan with the provider. Getting ready for work and surviving her shift sapped her of all her strength. Since the endless supply of casseroles had run out, she had found herself eating fast food, unable to summon up the willpower needed to make weekly trips to the grocery store. It really didn't matter though. Food had lost its flavor now that Robert was gone. She ate to survive, not completely caring about that too much either, but she couldn't escape the feeling that her husband would want her to go on, so she did. Even she couldn't deny that she was merely a shell of the person she had been only a few months ago.

"Kayleigh, how are you doing?" Looking up into the kind eyes of her boss, Kayleigh instantly felt tears forming in her own. When would the crying stop? Was it normal for the pain to feel as fresh today as it did on the day her husband died? And did her boss really want to know how she was doing? She doubted that anyone could handle her answer if she were to be honest about how she was really feeling. She knew she didn't have the energy to deal with any of it, so she never told anyone the truth.

Choosing to give the other woman an easy out, she smiled as she answered, "I'm holding up. Thanks for asking." Feeling herself flinch slightly as her boss squeezed her shoulder kindly before walking away, she wiped the sudden tears from her eyes, thinking about how rare it was for anyone to touch her anymore. She missed that. Missed Robert's hugs. Missed holding his hand. Just missed the way his skin felt when it was near hers. But she wouldn't be feeling that again, and she simply had to get her act together. She had clearly seen what was behind her boss's look. Her work was suffering, and she was sure the time would come for a much more serious talk between the two of them if she didn't figure out a way to pull it together.

What advice would Robert give me? Laughing out loud just a bit as she thought this, Kayleigh let her eyes close shut as she imagined him giving her one of his famous pep talks. Even though he had grown too old to play basketball competitively, he had still coached a team every chance he got. And he constantly talked to her like she was one of his players. Yes, he would tell her to toughen up, to move on, to pull it together. The smile left her face as she realized how impossible that all sounded. She knew, of course, that she had to move forward with her life. After all, you couldn't stay in one spot forever. But moving on implied not needing her husband anymore, and Kayleigh knew better than anyone that was just not going to happen.

She somehow got through the rest of her workday. When

it was finally time to stand up and grab her purse, she used her knee to push her chair closer to her desk. Once there was a carefully constructed smile pasted on her face, she turned around and made her way out of the office and toward her car. Maybe she would take her husband's advice and move forward a bit tonight. A trip to the grocery store sounded like a starting point. She would walk up and down the aisles, throwing enough into the cart to fill her cabinets at home. Then she would use some of whatever she ended up buying to finally cook a meal for herself, even if it was something as simple as a box of macaroni and cheese. She would do it for Robert, taking care not to notice the hollow sound of her bowl and fork as she placed them in the sink after she finished eating.

*

Getting ready for bed used to be a fun ritual, a pleasant way to wind down after a long day. Kayleigh smiled to herself as she remembered how she used to look forward to taking a hot bath before slipping into some comfy pajamas long before she was ready to climb into their bed. It was always her most relaxing time of day. Robert usually had a movie ready for them to watch even though they never made it through the whole thing without deciding to pause long enough to pop some popcorn. If she closed her eyes, she could smell the butter she had melted to add to the already greasy microwave popcorn they always kept in the pantry, could hear their laughter blending together as she reached over and asked for more out of his bowl. But her house was silent now, and she hadn't felt like snacking or watching a movie for quite some time.

Kayleigh climbed into bed without bothering to remove the comforter like she had done every other night of her adult life. Pushing her back up against the thick fabric, she decided she liked the way it felt against her body. She knew she was being pathetic, but she was desperate and wanted, needed, to at least pretend to have Robert in bed with her. Sitting up to roll the material a bit, she pushed around until she thought she had it perfect. Sighing as she laid her head back against her pillow, she scooted over until her body was pressed against the comforter again. She cried as she thought about how many times Robert had reached over to drape his arm around her before they both drifted off to sleep. She would give anything to feel the weight of his body against hers just one more time. The emptiness of their bed had been tormenting her night after night. Even though she knew how ridiculous she was being right now, she just didn't care. Maybe tonight she would be able to sleep without having any dreams.

Chapter Two

May 17, 2015

Robert regretted volunteering for this shift. Even though Kayleigh was at work too, he knew he would get home much later than she would. He couldn't get her off his mind today for some reason. Knowing he needed to focus on work right now, he settled for sending her a quick text before turning toward the fire truck. Even though the few words he managed to type out didn't say even a fraction of what was in his heart, he knew there was no time to think about it now. He had to leave his phone and all thoughts of his wife at the station. Turning his attention to the call that had just come in, he felt the familiar switch turn inside of him. It was time to focus on the task ahead. Hoping it would be an easy fire to deal with, he knew, as well as any firefighter, the risks that were involved every time they went out.

Offering up a quick prayer as they pulled up to the burning building a few minutes later, Robert jumped down from the truck and rushed toward the flames, knowing his crew was right there with him. As he ran into the building, his first thought was to head up the stairs to make sure no one was trapped on the second floor. Having done this dozens of times before, he mentally went through everything he knew he was about to experience. His goal, as always, was to be thorough while also being safe. He had never been out on a call without saving everyone, and he was determined today would be no different. Everyone on his crew had a role to play, and he was confident they were all as focused as he was.

Rounding a corner and entering what he could only assume was a bedroom, Robert sensed more than saw a figure near the window. As thick as the smoke was, he knew he didn't have much time to help whoever it was. As he approached the person, he didn't have time to react before he felt himself in what could only be described as an uncomfortable bear hug. He knew some people often panicked in times of distress, but this felt personal somehow. The other man didn't let go no matter how hard Robert tried to get away. As he tried to figure out why someone would grab him and push him, he felt his body twist as it made sudden contact with glass. He realized that his life was in danger, and unable to think quickly enough to determine why this was happening, he simply fought back with every bit of strength he had in him, all thoughts of saving the other man quickly leaving his mind. When the glass broke and he felt himself hanging out the window, his thoughts suddenly turned to his wife. He never could have predicted any of this, had never heard of anything like this happening to a firefighter. It certainly wasn't something he had been trained to deal with. Pushing back against the much stronger man, Robert felt himself losing the battle. The last thought that went through his mind as he flew through the air toward the paved parking lot below was of Kayleigh's beautiful face and how it would look when she found out he had left her. He was suddenly struck with regret as he thought of all the words he had left unsaid, all too aware of how big a mistake he had made by not saying them. The pain of his body breaking as it hit the ground mirrored the pain he felt in his heart as thoughts of life without his wife washed over him.

*

"Robbie? Can you hear me?" As Chief Preston said this, he felt tears form in his eyes. Robbie Wilson was more than just one of the most talented men on his crew; he was also his best friend. And things weren't looking too good for him right now. Even as he spoke words meant to reassure the other man, Chief knew they were most likely lies. He had seen a lot on this job, and everything told him his friend didn't have long to live.

Groaning more than talking, Robert tried to speak. He knew the fall had most likely cost him his life. He needed his best friend to listen to him carefully in case he never got the chance to tell Kayleigh everything he needed her to know. Grateful when Chief bent down close to his face, Robert whispered, "Please…"

"What is it, Robbie? What can I do?"

Wishing he could say more, but knowing he couldn't, he simply looked at his friend, hoping their shared memories would be enough for now. The pain was more than he could handle, making it impossible to focus on anything else.

Chief turned his head away for a moment, not wanting his tears to be seen by the only true friend he had ever known. His mind went back to many years ago when he had first met Robbie Wilson. They had become instant friends as little boys, and they now knew as much about each other as they knew about themselves. Grabbing his hand, Chief squeezed it lightly, wishing he could take away the other man's pain.

Hearing the paramedics approaching a few minutes later, he gave him one last sad look before backing away, allowing them the room they needed to do their job. He knew they were as upset as he was. Everyone loved the veteran firefighter, and he knew the paramedics, even as professional as they all were, would struggle to control their feelings as they worked to save their friend's life.

Shaking his head as he turned his back on the medical attention the paramedics were giving, he made his way over to the truck and the phone he would need to use to shatter the world of his best friend's wife. It wasn't a call he was looking forward to making even though he knew he was the only one who could make her understand. He could only hope she would have enough time to see her husband again, to hear the words he knew Robbie was desperate to tell her.

Chapter Three

Fall 2015

Kayleigh woke up startled. Pushing the comforter away before turning her head, she felt a soft cry slip past her lips as her eyes focused on the emptiness staring back at her. Why had all of this happened? She and Robert had thought they had all the time in the world. After their first conversation as lab partners in Professor Chandler's Biology 101 class, they had been inseparable. It had always amazed her how they had become best friends so quickly. She allowed her crying to turn into laughter as she considered how slow they had both been to discover that their feelings ran much deeper than just friends. Even so, getting married right after graduation had seemed as natural as breathing. An orphan, Kayleigh was accepted by Robert's parents as another one of their children, the daughter they had always longed for. The love she had felt from them had helped heal her from a lifetime of pain and fill the void that she had felt since childhood. Losing both of them in a car accident a few years back had crushed her as much as it had Robert. And now she was all alone, without a family to help her grieve.

Staring up at the ceiling, Kayleigh listened to the silence that seemed to follow her around the house. This house that used to be full of laughter. She missed the sound of her husband's voice. She missed their silly inside jokes. She missed everything she had thought would never go away. She missed the way life used to be. The silence deafened her, often bringing her to her knees, her hands quickly going up seemingly on their own to cover her ears in vain. She knew the echoes of voices she was trying to shield herself from weren't actually there, but the silence made them louder than she could explain. In it, in the cacophony of forgotten conversations, sometimes she felt like running away from her house just to get away from it all. Most of all, she simply hated being alone.

Forcing herself out of bed, Kayleigh looked down at the plush carpet and frowned as she noticed how clean it was. She couldn't believe she missed Robert's messes. What she wouldn't give to complain again about picking up a bunch of dirty socks off the floor. It reminded her of how sad she had been the first time they had noticed there wasn't any dog hair on their carpet anymore, dog hair that had stuck to the bottoms of their socks for as long as she could remember. Hands on her hips, she wondered if maybe she should get another dog now. Since their chocolate lab had died three years ago, they had been putting off getting another one. Neither she nor Robert could stand the thought of replacing Max. They had always joked that she was the only child they ever needed, neither one willing to discuss the fact that they were never able to have a real one of their own despite trying for over a decade. They had never wanted to get tested, choosing to trust the Lord to give them a child if He saw fit. Kayleigh now fiercely regretted their decision to not at least take a few tests or try to adopt. Maybe having a son or daughter to reach out to right now would lessen her pain somehow. Deciding not to dwell on a decision long ago buried, she walked to the bathroom to begin another day. They all seemed to roll together now. She would do what she had to and get through this one like she had all the others since the day her husband had died. And when it mercifully came to an end, she would go to sleep, only to start it all over again tomorrow. The thought of days turning into weeks, months, and then years almost caused her knees to buckle. How was she going to get through this life without Robert?

*

Kayleigh threw her purse on the couch with a little more force than was necessary. She knew she needed to get her emotions under control, but they were all over the place and she had no idea how to pull herself together. The day had started on a sour note and work certainly hadn't made it any better. None of the pep talks she imagined hearing from her husband had helped her this time. She wasn't sure if anything ever would again.

Sitting beside her purse on the otherwise empty couch, she glanced at the pile of stuff on the coffee table. When Chief had brought over Robert's belongings from his work locker, she had refused to look at, much less touch, any of it. And so he had left it on the table where it had been gathering dust for the past several weeks. Sighing deeply, she scooted to the edge of the cushions to get a better look at what her husband had left behind at the station he had always lovingly called his home away from home. Seeing his cell phone made her breath catch. Picking it up carefully, she wasn't surprised to discover the battery had died. She knew she could plug it in, wait a bit, and find herself back in her husband's world. But she was afraid to do it, afraid because she knew this was her final link to him. Just the thought of seeing his texts and looking at his history from the day he died made her instantly exhausted, feeling as though the weight of it all would crush her. She knew, after this, there would be no other piece of her husband for her to hold in her hands. He would forever only be in her heart.

Standing up, she sighed as she went to look for a charger. It was time to move forward, and if that meant stepping back in time briefly then so be it. After she plugged the phone in, Kayleigh made her way to the kitchen to peer into the fridge.

Pulling out a tub of chicken salad, she decided to toast some rye bread to go with it. It was a far cry from the elaborate meals she and Robert had made together in this kitchen night after night. In fact, as she glanced around her, she realized she no longer needed most of the appliances they had used. Maybe she should have a yard sale. Maybe getting rid of stuff that reminded her of her husband would help ease some of her pain. Deciding she was willing to try anything, she settled at the table with her meager meal and pulled out her phone to take a few notes. Yes, maybe a yard sale would help her clean out the house a bit. There was too much of Robert hanging around, reminding her of what she couldn't have anymore. She certainly didn't need the space, but she somehow knew the emptiness a yard sale would provide would fill the house more than all of her husband's clothes and belongings did. The memories were weighing her down, and she didn't know how much more weight she could bear before she collapsed.

Cleaning up what passed for her supper only took a few minutes. Kayleigh kicked off her shoes as she made her way back to where she had left Robert's phone. Hoping the charger had done its job, she dared to push the button that would turn on the home screen. And just like that, before she had time to mentally prepare for what she was about to see, there was a picture of a happy memory staring up at her. She smiled as she thought about what they had been doing when Robert had held his phone out to capture this shot of the two of them. They had been at the end of a long hike, and both looked tired and sweaty and deliriously happy. It had been a good day, but all days spent with her husband had been wonderful. She couldn't lose sight of the perfect life they had been blessed to enjoy together, no matter what today felt like.

Looking at a picture was one thing, but taking the next step made Kayleigh's breath catch. She knew this was her one chance to enter Robert's life again. Looking at his history would tell her what he had been doing that last day. Reading all his text messages would let her know who had been on his mind. And then, even though she hated to admit it, she would know all she would ever know about her husband.

Deciding to read his texts first, Kayleigh almost dropped the phone when she found the unsent one. Robert must have typed it out in a rush. Why else wouldn't he have sent it?

"Babe I'm headed out on a call but I just can't get you out of my head. Do you know how much I love you?"

Kayleigh couldn't breathe for a moment. It felt as though he had stepped into the room, gathered her up in his arms, and whispered those words for her ears only. Reading them again, she bowed her head to thank God for giving her this precious and unexpected gift.

Thoughts of looking at anything else on the phone left her mind. Reaching under the coffee table to where she kept some books, she grabbed her journal and a pen. Even though there was no way she would ever forget what Robert had written to her in his final text, she wanted to write the words down. Opening the journal to reveal the front cover, she carefully wrote down every word, almost hearing his voice as she did so. It comforted her in a way she had not thought possible since his horrible accident.

Settling back against the pillows on her couch, she grabbed one to hold against her chest. Looking down at it, she remembered when Robert had helped her pick it out while they were on one of their lazy Saturday morning road trips. She smiled as she thought about how they had been trying to freshen up the room in an attempt to avoid spending money on a new couch even though they desperately needed to replace their old one. Putting the pillow aside, she grabbed the journal again and held it to her chest, almost hugging it like she wished she could hug Robert just one last time. *Thank you, Babe. You just don't know how much I needed to hear that right now.*

Deciding to celebrate, Kayleigh set aside the journal and headed toward the kitchen. She would pop some popcorn tonight, pick out a movie, and snuggle under a blanket on the couch just like they used to do together. Maybe tomorrow she would find the strength to move on a bit more. Robert would be proud of her, proud of her baby steps. He had always told her that if you're moving, you're making progress. If his advice had been true for his basketball teams, why couldn't it work for her too?

Chapter Four

Kayleigh looked around the closet. *What in the world am I going to do with all this space?* Trying her best not to imagine her husband's clothes hanging on the now-empty rods, she forced herself to focus on her side of the closet. Well, what used to be her side. It was all hers now. As her hand quickly went up to cover the sad sound trying to make its way past her lips, she felt her legs refuse to hold her up anymore. Landing on her knees, she wasn't surprised when deep heaving sobs overtook her. After several minutes, when it was becoming a little challenging to take a breath, she rolled over onto her side, curling her body into a tight ball. *Oh, Robert! I just don't know if I can survive. I never knew pain could feel like this.* Letting her mind go blank, she eventually drifted off to sleep.

Waking up a few hours later, she slowly opened her eyes and smiled, still feeling the residue of her dream. She gasped as she continued to feel his fingers as they gently brushed across her cheeks. *Robert? Are you here?* Even as she allowed herself to think it, the joy she had been feeling quickly turned sour. She knew her husband was gone, was never coming back. It had just been a dream; that's all. So very real, but still just something dredged up by her subconscious. It was almost a cruel trick. Waking up from the dream made the life she used to have, her life with her husband, seem even more lost than ever.

Kayleigh sat up, forcing herself to look at the empty side of their closet again. This time she thought about how easy it would be to remove the rods and add several shelves. Yes, she could finally get her sweaters out of the dresser drawers that were much too small to hold them all. She could use this space. And maybe one day she could walk into this closet without being assaulted by memories of Robert. Maybe one day she would be able to truly let him go.

*

Suffering in silence day after day was a level of loneliness she hadn't known existed before her husband had died. Kayleigh found herself lying to everyone around her. She knew they all meant well, but how could she answer honestly when someone asked her how she was? The truth was too horrifying to articulate, so she lied. And watching the relief flit across each of their faces made Kayleigh shrink further into herself, alone with the silence.

"Kayleigh? You home?"

Hearing her friend at the front door forced her off the couch. She checked her face in the mirror before attempting a smile. Opening the door, she felt tears form as she recognized pity in her best friend's eyes.

"I'm not good company right now, but I'm glad you stopped by."

As Becca put her arms around her friend, she pushed the door shut behind them with her foot before saying, "I sort of thought you might need someone to talk to this morning. Or not. If you just want me to sit with you and listen, I can do that too. We can even sit and not talk at all. Seriously, whatever you need. I just want you to know I'm here for you."

As they settled on the couch beside each other, Kayleigh took a deep breath before turning to her friend and admitting, "How many pieces can my heart be broken into? There's always a layer of sadness underneath everything I think, everything I say, everything I do. I continue to put one foot in front of the other because it's what I have to do. It's what Robert would have wanted me to do, but it's just so hard. I still feel him with me, but I can't touch him. The pain is excruciating, and the worst part is I know it won't ever end. How am I supposed to learn to live with the pain, to live without Robert?" Kayleigh paused long enough to look up into her best friend's face. She immediately felt guilt wash over her for dumping so much emotion on someone else. She just couldn't keep these feelings in a moment longer though, so she went on, "He's everywhere, but he's not here. I dream about him. I mean, I have unbelievably realistic dreams about him, but he's not in them. I mean he's in them, but it's not my

Robert. Man, I'm not making any sense." When her friend reached out to squeeze her shoulder, Kayleigh took a deep breath and finished with, "Robert's with me. He is with me. And knowing that's almost worse than losing him. I'm just not sure what I'm supposed to do with him now."

Risking another look at her friend, she was relieved to see only sadness in Becca's eyes. She knew she was rambling, not making much sense, but Becca was the kind of friend who would do as she promised and just listen. And, after all, that really was all she needed right now. Knowing better than to reveal the depth of her dreams to anyone, even her best friend, she stood up and hugged her before walking across the room to grab a few tissues they both needed.

Wiping her own tears away, Becca softly said, "I don't know what you're feeling, but I kinda think it's a blessing you still feel Robert with you. I know it doesn't take away the pain, and I know nothing will ever replace him being here, but maybe whatever this is will help you grieve? I'm so sorry. I love you so much and hate to see you in pain. I know one thing though, Robert adored you. I'm just so sorry about everything."

"Thanks." Kayleigh took a minute to compose herself before saying, "Let's go to the kitchen. I baked like a crazy lady last night." Pausing to let out a soft laugh that didn't reach her eyes, she added, "I made all of Robert's favorites even though I don't have much of an appetite these days. How about we sample a little bit of everything?"

Putting her arms around her friend's shoulders, Becca smiled as she groaned a little before saying, "Sure, bring on the calories!"

Both women forced themselves to fill their plates with sugary goodness that didn't tempt either of them. Switching the subject to something safe, they ate while they made small talk about the aspects of their lives that really didn't matter much to Kayleigh anymore. Discussing the newest movie and the latest shade of lipstick seemed like a safe way to end their visit even though both had so much more on their minds.

Becca wondered how to help her friend while Kayleigh longed for another night with Robert, even if she could only be with him in her dreams.

Chapter Five

Kayleigh woke up confused and, as odd as it felt even to her, happier than she had been since the day Robert had died. This dream did more than linger in her thoughts. As she felt the coolness of the pillow under her head, she hummed a line from a song she had been listening to in her sleep. She had been dancing with Robert at their wedding, but the strange thing was that it had been during the traditional mother-son dance, a dance she definitely hadn't shared with her new husband years ago on their special day. She had looked up into his eyes and felt an overwhelming sense of love combined with pride. It had shaken her to her core in the dream, and she continued to feel it in its fullness now that she was awake. She was experiencing the happiness of a mother, a feeling she had certainly never felt before. As she pondered the meaning behind it all, something she found herself doing a lot lately, she felt a closeness to her mother-in-law that she had never felt in real life even though they had been more like mother and daughter than in-laws. She understood the woman so much better right now than she had ever thought possible before. Tears slipped from her eyes, wetting her pillowcase, as she tried to wrap her head around the kind of love she was feeling. It was a love that would allow her to gladly lay down her life for someone else. A love that stirred up happiness while letting go of someone you love more than your own life, even while gladly handing him over to another. As she realized what Robert's mom had given up that day, and the way she had so lovingly shared him with her, she loved the woman more than ever. At their wedding, she had thought the dance between the two of them was sweet. Now, she realized it had been good-bye. As Robert held his mom in his arms that night, Kayleigh now realized how her mother-in-law had felt so many emotions in that one moment: the weight of carrying a newborn, the thrill of having a toddler crawl onto her lap just to be held, and the joy of feeling a young boy's arms wrapped around her in a hug. She had felt it all, all while sharing one last dance with her son. That dance had been a final chance to have her son to herself. And, as Kayleigh felt her sobs deepen, she finally recognized how giving him away had been her mother-in-law's silent wedding present to her. The other woman had let Robert go that day, and Kayleigh finally understood the cost. Closing her eyes, she allowed herself to travel back to the dream one more time, remembering how it had felt to see such pure love reflected back in her husband's eyes. She had always known he loved his parents, but now she fully understood the depth of that love.

Opening her eyes, Kayleigh threw her legs over the side of the bed, forcing her body to lift. She got up so quickly that she instantly felt a wave of dizziness try to push her back down onto the bed. Fighting the uncomfortable feeling, she forced herself to walk to the bathroom where she could stare at her reflection in the mirror. Yes, she was still the same woman she had been when she had fallen asleep last night. The woman she had been in the dream was definitely not staring back, but she couldn't shake the feeling that she was still somehow with her. Instead of unsettling her, it offered a strange sort of comfort.

Knowing someone else had loved her husband as much as she had was something she needed to feel right now. Even if she didn't understand the dream, and why she had become Robert's mom in it, she was grateful. Feeling the love only a mother could feel for a child sent waves of happiness through her. For the first time in a long time, Kayleigh looked forward to starting her day. She hoped the feeling would hang around, maybe even replace the dark place she veered toward so often lately.

*

Glancing at her full to-do list did nothing to dampen her mood when she finally got to work later that morning. Sitting down at her desk, she was surprised that she didn't feel the heaviness she had been feeling for so long. Toe tapping, Kayleigh let out a tiny giggle as she resisted the urge to spin her chair around in circles. She knew it was the dream that was making her feel so good even while she knew none of it was real. The lightness she felt in her chest was so welcome that she didn't care why she was feeling it. Maybe it all really was a gift from Robert, but even if it was just a trick of her tired mind, she welcomed it. She needed a break from the pain she had been carrying around, and she could only hope the feeling would last.

Wearing a smile that felt good on her face, Kayleigh worked through the morning without taking any breaks. When her lunch hour rolled around, she felt strong enough to do something she had been putting off since the accident. Seeing the fire station come into view a few minutes later didn't take the spring out of her step. She breathed a sigh of relief as she looked up and whispered thanks to her husband. Other people might think she was crazy, and she was okay with that, but Robert felt so real to her right now, how could she not talk to him?

"Kayleigh, what brings you down here?" Chief's smile did little to hide the hint of sadness in his voice. Kayleigh felt herself falter for the first time all day as she considered the depth of her husband's best friend's pain.

"Chief, I just wanted to come by and thank you in person.

The stuff from Robert's locker, especially his phone, meant the world to me. I really appreciate you making sure I got it all."

"Of course." Chief hesitantly reached out to hug her, pulling back just enough to look into her eyes as he continued, "Is there anything, anything at all, I can do? I know Robbie would want me to take care of you, but I honestly don't know what you need."

Watching Chief run a trembling hand through what little hair was left on his head made Kayleigh's heart squeeze in her chest. This man had been a true friend to her husband. It made her smile to remember all the times he had come to their home for a game night or to cook on the grill with them.

"I'm good. Actually I'm better today than I've been in a long time. I just wanted to pop in and see you, maybe some of the guys. It seemed like something Robert would want me to do."

Chief pointed toward the kitchen where Kayleigh could hear a fairly heated card game being played before asking, "Why don't you let me fix you a cup of tea? You can visit with the guys. Maybe they'll even tone it down a bit if you're in there. I was just about to break up their game before someone said something they would regret later."

Kayleigh enjoyed hearing the slight chuckle in his voice. It was good to be back in the place Robert had loved so much. He had told her many times how he had wanted to be a firefighter since he was a young boy. After college, he made that dream his reality, putting his business degree in a frame to hang on their office wall at home instead of using it. She knew he had pursued it as a gift to his parents and she had always loved him for being that kind of son, but his heart had been in this fire station. She knew he loved helping those in need, loved being part of a team, and even enjoyed the thrill of danger. She felt her smile fade just a little as she considered the irony of it all.

Shaking her head slightly to remove any unpleasant thoughts before they gained a foothold, Kayleigh felt her smile grow bigger as she watched each man, one at a time, stand up and move toward her. As they surrounded her, she felt nothing but love as they embraced her in one of the best group hugs she had ever experienced. She knew Robert would be proud of all of them and that he would have been the first to stand up from the table if she had been one of their wives instead of his.

When they offered her a place at the table, she declined, explaining she had to get back to the office. Seeing them, if only for a few minutes, had made her feel closer to Robert somehow. Making sure to look each of them in the eye, she wondered why one of the younger men looked away so quickly. She didn't recognize his face. Glancing at the name on his uniform brought a small smile to her own face as she remembered conversations Robert had shared with her. This young man, Trent Jefferson, was someone her husband had taken under his wing. The two men had worked out at the gym together, and her husband had always enjoyed telling her stories about the younger firefighter. There were times he was frustrated with the other man. She hadn't known what kind of issues Trent had been working through, but it had made her proud to know her husband was willing to spend time with a rookie just to help him with whatever problems he had. It was just one more reason she had loved everything about Robert Wilson.

As she walked out of the station with Chief by her side, holding the tea he had graciously fixed for her in a to-go cup, she asked the one question that had been bothering her since the day the fire had claimed her husband. "Chief, who went in with Robert that last call?"

"Oh Kayleigh, I was hoping you wouldn't ask that. He feels so bad, like he let Robbie down. It was Trent Jefferson. I'm not sure if you ever met him; he was the young fellow in there who didn't have a lot to say. Real quiet kid, that one. Robbie was sort of a father figure to him, and the kid has been taking what happened real hard." Reaching out to touch her shoulder lightly, he continued softly, "Trust me, we just finished our investigation, and everything checks out. As hard as it is to believe, all the evidence points to Robbie getting disoriented that night. I can't make sense out of how he fell out of that window like he did, but we are just gonna have to chalk it up to a freak accident."

Wiping away the tears that had fallen down her face without her even being aware of them, Kayleigh hugged the man again as she whispered, "I never even considered it was anything other than an accident. I hope Trent's okay. Robert talked about him enough that I know he thought the world of him. He sure did love to help people, didn't he?" Looking up again at her husband's friend, Kayleigh wasn't surprised to see tears slip out of his eyes and onto his cheeks too.

"You know, he really did take that kid under his wing. That's another reason I hate that he was Robbie's partner that night. It's a good thing he's young because it will take him a long time to get over what happened."

"Give him my best?"

Chief smiled as he said, "You bet. Robbie would be so proud of you, you know that, right?"

Kayleigh nodded softly in answer before she walked away. She knew she had a little less spring in her step as she walked back to work, but she was glad she had made this trip. Yes, her husband would be proud of her. She had moved a little more in the right direction like he would have wanted her to. She just wished she could have talked to Trent. It would be good to give him a hug and tell him none of this was his fault. She would find a way to reach out to him. It's what Robert would want her to do.

Chapter Six

Kayleigh was getting used to the way her life seemed to swing from welcome highs to unbearable lows, both entering her day with almost no warning. Although she was grateful to be enjoying more happy days than sad ones, she still struggled when the sadness tried to overtake her. She didn't need a therapist to tell her that what she was experiencing was normal, even though she had a sinking feeling this was going to be what her normal was going to feel like from now on. How could she expect to get over losing the love of her life? And, if she were being honest, she didn't want to stop feeling the pain. Not completely. Somehow feeling bad made her feel a bit more alive. As much as all of this made sense to her, it was not something she felt comfortable sharing with anyone else.

Opening the mail after work made her voice catch as she uttered a small cry before tears started pouring down her face. She had known the insurance check would arrive eventually, but seeing it and holding it in her hands was almost more than she could take. How could she cash it? Her husband's life was being reduced to a dollar sign and it sickened her.

Stumbling as she walked toward one of the kitchen chairs, Kayleigh had her head on the table almost before she fully sat down. Knowing it was what Robert wanted for her helped a little with the pain. They had discussed his life insurance policy on more than one occasion, and she was proud that he had provided so well for her. Even though she knew Robert would want her to have the money, everything in her wanted to rip the check into a million tiny pieces before throwing away the awful evidence of his death.

Putting it down for the time being, she got up, thinking a shower might help, and made her way upstairs to her bathroom. Standing under the steaming flow of water a few minutes later, she was surprised when the tears just wouldn't stop. She couldn't help but feel like Robert was with her, putting his arms around her and telling her everything was going to be okay. She knew he would want her to use the money to make her life a little easier just like she knew every penny spent would remind her of all she had lost.

Reaching up to turn off the water a little while later, she stood there with her eyes closed before whispering softly, "Babe, I know you can't hear me, but I need to say this anyway. I miss you. I had no idea how much I would miss you. Please, please help me make sense of all of this."

Feeling more than a little silly at her outburst, Kayleigh grabbed a towel from the shelf beside the shower and dried herself off. She knew she needed to get dressed, force herself to eat something, and maybe do a little housework. Just because this wasn't what she would call one of her good days, life didn't give her the luxury of wallowing in her sadness. She knew she had to keep moving, but it wasn't long before she gave in to the desire to curl up in a ball under her thick comforter.

*

Opening her eyes didn't help a bit. It took a moment to adjust to the darkness before she reached for her phone on the bedside table. Looking at it, she was surprised to see it was just a few minutes past 11:00. Somehow she felt refreshed and exhausted at the same time. Like before, this dream had been so real, but this time she didn't wake up feeling the lightness she had after the last one. This one bothered her more than a little, and she knew she would need some time to process it. Robert's face kept blurring in her mind. She wanted to see him, but something was keeping him out of focus.

Throwing the covers off in frustration, she quickly got out of bed and made her way downstairs. Thinking a cup of tea might calm her nerves, she filled the kettle with water and placed it on the stove. Reaching for the purple cup trimmed with yellow and white flowers that had been her favorite for as long as she could remember, she startled herself by almost dropping it. Putting it on the counter where it would be safe, she held her hands together in an attempt to stop them from trembling. Once she felt like she was a little more under control, she found a box of tea bags and added one to the cup. Pouring the now-hot water, she stared as the clear liquid started to darken. She normally would slice a lemon to add to it, but tonight she didn't think she had the energy.

Deciding to take her cup of comfort into the living room, she curled up on the couch before finally allowing herself to remember the dream. It had been real enough to almost scare her. She had seen her husband as a young child this time, and while seeing him that way was delightful, it also was a sad reminder of the child they were never allowed to have.

*

"Robbie, let me see what you're working on."

When Robbie heard his teacher call his name, his head jerked up and he stared at her for just a minute before feeling his face stretch into a big smile. Wanting to please her, he answered, "I was drawing a butterfly. I saw one fly by outside the window when we were working on our spelling words. It was so pretty. I wanted to try to color it exactly the same color so I can show it to my momma after school." Holding the half-finished drawing up to show Miss Corbett, Robbie held his breath. He liked his pretty teacher, and he sure did want to make her happy.

Bending down to look at his picture before looking into his wide eyes, she found herself lost in the kindness she saw there. She gasped as she thought about how they still looked the same, then slowly stood up when she realized the eyes she remembered so well were permanently closed now. Forcing a smile, she added, "Robbie, I think your mom will be very happy to see that butterfly. Good job, Buddy."

Kayleigh walked away quickly, needing to find a mirror. This was so weird. Her husband, or the child her husband used to be, clearly thought she was his teacher. How old was he? She certainly didn't know a lot about children, but she knew he couldn't be older than five or six. Oh, but he sure had been a cute child! Seeing him made her realize she had never seen any pictures of her husband at this age. She pondered this for a second, and then let it go as she realized she didn't have time to waste thinking about her mother-in-law's lack of scrapbooking skills.

"Miss Corbett? Can you come help me?" Hearing Robbie's voice again made Kayleigh look around the room. How was he the only child in the classroom? When she heard his high little voice start to make a sound that seemed more like whining than speaking, she quickly walked toward his desk again.

"What do you need? Are you working on another picture for your mom?"

When the little boy smiled at her this time, it was so sweet that Kayleigh thought her heart would break from happiness. He obviously wanted to please her; she could see his little hands shaking a bit as he waited to see her response.

"This heart you drew is so pretty. I know R.W. stands for your name, but what about the other initials? Does your mom's name start with a K? Is that why you put K.W. in the heart too?"

When Robbie looked up at her this time, Kayleigh's hands immediately found their way to her chest. She wasn't seeing the smile of a little boy anymore. Somehow, even though she was still seeing a child in front of her, she clearly was looking into the face of her husband. The way the lines around his eyes crinkled as he stared at her, the way his face turned to the side just a little as he gave her that look that always made her want to be closer to him, the way she heard his deep throaty laugh start to rumble right before he spoke to her, everything made her all too aware that she was in the presence of the love of her life.

She was bending down toward him when she woke up. And now she was left trying to figure out the dream. Even though she had known, even while she was sleeping, that the child she was looking at didn't really know who she was, she had somehow been given a gift, a glimpse of her husband, the man she had never thought she would see again. That didn't stop the dream from confusing her though.

She needed to tell someone about it, but the dream sounded crazy even to her. How could she explain it so someone else would take her seriously? She just wasn't sure she could take the risk, and to be honest, part of her was enjoying keeping Robert to herself.

Chapter Seven

January 2015

Robert couldn't stop feeling like something was trying to pull him under. He had thought Chief was calling him into his office to offer a promotion that would come with not only more responsibility but also a pay increase, both highly coveted by him. He couldn't have been more wrong. When he finished hearing everything his friend had to say, Robert took a few seconds to compose himself before attempting an answer.

"So, you want me to take this new kid under my wing? Even though we both know that everything in his file points to him not being capable of doing any job, much less this one? Help me understand why you think this kid would be a match for me? Or why I would be able to help him? I'm a little lost here."

Chief blew out his breath before answering his friend. He was about to open an old wound, and even though he knew it might be a good thing in the long run, today was going to bring back pain that Robert couldn't possibly have seen coming.

Looking directly at him before speaking, Chief finally said, "Remember Meghan?" Settling back into his chair as he watched the expression on the other man's face turn from surprise to anger to grief, he waited to hear what he would say.

"Yeah." Buying a few seconds by rubbing his hand through his hair, Robert continued, "You know I do. Please enlighten me about all of this though. How is this guy connected to Meghan?"

"I think he might be her little brother."

Robert ran his hand over his face slowly before lowering it to reveal the grimace Chief wished he didn't have to see before adding, "You have to be kidding me. I barely remember her family, other than her sister of course. Did she even have a little brother? How in the world did he end up here?"

Chief sighed as he answered, "I have no idea. I don't even know if the kid knows who you are. I wouldn't have even known who he was if I hadn't read his file so thoroughly. That essay, you know? For whatever reason, I actually read his and, well, he mentioned a few names, and Meghan's name was one of them, and, you know, so I figured it out real quick like."

Standing up as he answered, Robert said, "I don't have a choice about this, do I?"

Chief stood and walked around his desk so he could grab his friend around the shoulders before telling him, "You know if you do this then something good can come out of what happened, right?"

Robert's smile wasn't genuine when he answered, "Yeah, right. Look, Kayleigh doesn't know about any of this. Let's keep it all between the two of us, okay? I don't want to reveal myself to Meghan's brother either. Let me take care of him, maybe even help him figure out he won't make a good firefighter, and then we'll all be on our way. Sound good?"

As the two men walked out of the office, anyone watching would have clearly known that something serious had just happened. But no one would ask. Every man in the station knew that what happened in Chief's office stayed in Chief's office.

*

Trent had to admit he was out of his element, although he refused to give up. When Chief had called him into his office to explain that he would be working with Robert Wilson, he had fought hard to control the smile fighting to cover his face. The older man had an incredible reputation, and there was no one else he would have chosen to work with. But he had played it cool that day, leaving his boss's office without giving away even a hint of how he was really feeling.

Once they started working together though, he struggled. He didn't want to mess anything up, but everything the other man asked him to do seemed impossible. He had known when he had first started training to be a firefighter that he would need to work hard, but nothing had prepared him for the drills he was being put through now. Robert seemed to make scenarios up just as a new form of torture. Trent understood, deep down, that the veteran firefighter was helping him, but some days he could barely make it to his bed when he got home. He didn't realize a person's body could be so sore. Thankful for his natural size and the many hours he had put in at the gym to build his muscles, he still wondered on more than one occasion if strength alone would be enough to do this job.

It was more than just the physical work too. Robert was a thinker, and some of his drills felt more like IQ tests to Trent than the work that would one day help him put out a fire. But he was determined, and he soon almost started to feel like one of the guys. He could only hope his mentor would begin to see him as someone more than the pest Chief had straddled him with.

"Okay, Trent, that's it for today. You did good."

Looking down a bit so he could see into the other man's eyes, he was pleased to see a hint of a smile there. He gathered his thoughts before responding with, "Thanks. I don't know about you, but I'm beat."

Laughing while raising his arms above his head in an obviously painful stretch, Robert told the younger man, "You're beat, huh? Wait until you have about twenty more years under your belt. You don't know what sore feels like yet."

"Twenty years? Just how young do you think I am?"

Studying the other man for several seconds, Robert laughed again as he admitted, "I don't know why I said that. I'm actually a terrible judge of ages. I just know you're younger than me, so you don't know the same pain I'm feeling."

"Fair enough. Look, I'm gonna hit the shower and head out if we're done here?"

"Right there with you. And who knows? We might just make a firefighter out of you yet."

As both men walked toward the showers together, Trent felt happy. Maybe, for the first time in a long time, life would work out the way he planned. He sure was due for something good to come his way. If he played his cards right, all his hard work might just pay off.

Chapter Eight

Fall 2015

Kayleigh hadn't seen Robert at all in last night's dream, but she had still known he was there. In some ways he was more real this time than in all her other dreams, but she also couldn't shake the feeling that she had just spent time with a stranger, a man she certainly didn't know. She was unable to put her finger on what it was about this dream that bothered her so much, but she had the sudden urge to go take a shower, to wash the uncomfortable feeling off her skin.

*

September 1990

"Do you think he'll call?" as she asked this, the young girl put a finger in her mouth and started to chew on her nail. It was impossible not to see the fear in her blue eyes, and something else, something that could only be described as dangerous excitement.

Another girl, who looked so much like the first one that

there was no denying their relationship, answered her sister with a smile, "Sarah, why wouldn't he call you?"

"Why would he? I mean, we barely know each other. Maybe I'm just kidding myself. I mean why would a senior be interested in a freshman anyway? He has all those cute cheerleaders throwing themselves all over him after every basketball game. I was an idiot to give him my phone number when he asked for it. It was probably all a big joke to him."

"Do me a favor? Look in the mirror." Walking with her sister to the oval mirror they often fought over on school mornings, Meghan pushed the other girl's hair away from her face as she continued, "Sarah, you're gorgeous. Any guy would want to go out with you. Why are you surprised that Robbie Wilson asked for your number? He's going to call you, and he's going to ask you out. And Mom and Dad are going to freak out. If you want something to worry about, you need to worry about how you're going to get them to let you go anywhere with a guy that old."

Turning away from the mirror and throwing herself on the

bed they shared most nights, Sarah grabbed a fuzzy pink pillow and used it to stifle the squeal she just had to let out. Glancing up at her younger sister, she smiled as she said, "Do you really think so? Man, I would give anything to go on just one date with him. He's the most beautiful man I've ever laid eyes on."

"Beautiful, huh? Well, if you do go out with him, don't call him beautiful, you goofball! Just wait. The phone will ring any minute. You better hope Dad doesn't answer before we do. He'll scare Robbie off for sure."

Rolling onto her back, Sarah allowed herself to imagine what it would be like if he did call. What it would be like to get dressed up for him. Where they might go on their first date. She smiled as she thought about kissing him. Yes, she wanted him to call her. Even if her parents didn't think she was old enough to date, she knew she was ready. And the star basketball player would be the perfect guy to help her prove everyone wrong.

*

As Kayleigh downed the last drops from her teacup, she still couldn't shake the bad feeling that had been with her since her dream had jarred her suddenly awake. Pushing strands of damp hair away from her face, she still felt everything Sarah had been feeling in her dream, but there was more. It was like she was still caught up in the nervous excitement of liking a boy for the first time, a normal experience for every young girl and one she vividly remembered feeling so long ago, but there was more, something else lurking just beneath the surface. She couldn't quite put her finger on it, but something was making her feel very uncomfortable.

Giving up on analyzing the dream, Kayleigh made her way back up the stairs. Her husband, in the twenty-five years they had known each other, had certainly never mentioned a girlfriend named Sarah, and she was sure there had been no secrets between them. She didn't know why her brain had created this girl, but she simply was too tired to think about it anymore. As much as she believed her other dreams had been a gift, this one didn't feel like one. She shook her head as she thought about the tricks a person's brain could play; she was sure this was what was going on with her tonight.

Climbing back into bed, she fluffed the pillows and hoped the rest of the night would be dream-free. As much as she had enjoyed dancing with Robert at their wedding and seeing him as an adorable little boy, this time something felt off. It was almost like she woke up feeling a little bit afraid of her husband, a feeling which couldn't have been more ridiculous. One thing she knew for certain was that there had never been a kinder person than her Robert. Closing her eyes, she prayed for sleep to come, the kind that didn't allow dreams in.

*

When Kayleigh woke up the next morning, she stretched her arms above her head before slowly getting out of bed. Determined to remember how much her husband had meant to her, she thought back to before they had gotten married, to when Robert had been her boyfriend, not quite her husband yet.

"Mrs. Wilson, I don't know what you add to your food, but everything you make tastes so good!"

A smile creeping across her face, Sally Wilson chided her future daughter-in-law as she answered, "Kayleigh Ann, how many times do I have to remind you to call me Mom? You're a part of this family, and no child of mine's gonna get away with calling me Mrs. Wilson."

Feeling a slight blush heat her face, Kayleigh replied, "I keep forgetting. Mom and Dad are words I've never used in my life, but I sure am glad to have the chance to say them now. Thanks for reminding me."

Feeling strong fingers squeeze her own beneath the table where no one could see, Kayleigh was grateful for the man sitting beside her. Not only had he made her happier than she ever thought possible, but he had made her part of his amazing family. She had gotten her hopes up so many times, thinking she had a chance at having a forever family, but something always seemed to happen, causing her to get bumped into yet another home. She had lived her life on an emotional roller coaster, not quite belonging anywhere. Going away to college had made her feel almost normal except on visitation days when, from a distance, she watched her friends and their parents together. Meeting Robert had been a balm to her soul, and when their friendship had grown into something more, she finally felt at home.

"Robbie, take our girl into the den, okay? I'll call you kids when the dessert is ready."

Smiling at the way his mom found a way to bring up the childhood nickname he wasn't fond of anymore, he winked at her. Even if Kayleigh didn't have a clue, he had been in this family long enough to know what a trip to the den after dinner really meant. There was more to this dessert than just something sweet to eat. His mom knew Kayleigh's birthday was coming up in a few days, and he had no doubt that she had something special planned for his girl. He wasn't sure if he had ever loved his mother as much as he did right now.

Once they were in the den, Kayleigh asked, "So, what's for dessert?"

Reaching down to tenderly kiss her instead of answering the question, Robert wished he had talked her into moving their wedding up a few months. What he wouldn't give to take her to their own home right now. But he knew it was important to let her plan the wedding of her dreams, and if that meant he had to wait a few extra months before she was truly his, then he could be patient.

"Robbie, huh? I guess you aren't going to answer me about dessert?"

"I honestly have no clue what Mom has planned, but I'm guessing it's not quite ready yet. Or maybe she wanted to give us some time alone. Yeah, that must be it. She could probably tell how hard it was for you to eat her pork chops and potatoes when all you could think about was kissing me."

"Hmmmm....so I was that obvious?" Instead of kissing him like he clearly wanted her to, she wrestled out of his arms and headed back toward the kitchen.

"Whoa there." Reaching her in a few short strides, Robert put his hands on her waist and pulled her to him again before saying, "I think Mom can handle whatever it is she's doing in there. I can give you something sweeter than whatever we're having for dessert." As his playful smile turned dangerously serious, he bent down, and with one hand wrapped in her long black hair, pulled her lips to his. Several seconds later, he pulled back far enough to stare into her eyes as he whispered, "Maybe you're right. We better go back in there with Mom and Dad. I don't trust myself to be alone with you right now."

When he reached down to hold her hand, Kayleigh could feel the way his trembled. She loved this man in a way she never knew was possible.

"Okay, you two."

Hearing his mom's cheerful voice, Robert told Kayleigh, "Let's go eat. And then we need to see if the folks want to play cards or something before you go home. I was serious. I honestly don't trust myself to be alone with you tonight."

Giving him a knowing smile, Kayleigh didn't bother with a response. Turning the corner and seeing the dessert Robert's mom had been working on made her stop in her tracks. There, in Sally Wilson's hands, was a cake covered in pink frosting and at least two dozen lit candles. None of them could possibly understand what was going on in her heart. She hadn't even shared with Robert the depth of sadness that had been her childhood. No one had ever made her a birthday cake before, and the emotion she was feeling right now swung from shock to sadness to joy. She was used to holding everything in, but tonight she desperately wanted to let these people, her family, know what this meant to her. But all she could do was smile as she told them thank you before following directions when told to blow out the candles to make a birthday wish. None of them would understand why she didn't make one though. They couldn't know that all her dreams had already come true.

Chapter Nine

March 2015

If Robert had to spend one more minute taking care of this kid he would scream. He understood why Chief had paired them together, just like he knew he had once been where Trent was at now, but it took every bit of patience he possessed to watch him make mistake after mistake. Rubbing his hand over his face, he took a few deep breaths. He needed to calm down. It wasn't Trent's fault that he was a rookie, but he wished he didn't have to be told how to do everything. Robert laughed a bit as he thought about his own lack of experience when he had first started out. He wasn't this bad, but he had certainly made his share of mistakes. He just had to figure out a way to give this rookie firefighter a break without risking anyone's life.

"Okay, Jefferson, one more time. I know you can do this. You just have to go through each step I taught you. No shortcuts this time, okay?"

And so it went. For more excruciating weeks than either of

them could count. And gradually, almost without Robert even realizing it, Trent stopped being a pest and started becoming one of the guys. It wasn't long before Robert was genuinely glad when he got a chance to work with the younger man. Their friendship never went beyond the fire station, but Robert still couldn't resist telling Kayleigh all about the younger firefighter.

"You won't believe what the goofball did today." Robert was talking to his wife before he was barely inside their front door. Kayleigh loved hearing the laughter in his voice. She was grateful they both had jobs they enjoyed, and it always made her happy to hear about the guys at the station. He talked about them so much that she felt like they were more like part of the family than friends. Although Chief came over and hung out with them quite a bit, somehow none of the other men from the station ever visited. She suspected that was Robert's way of protecting their time together. As much as he loved the guys, she knew he felt the same way about their time off that she did. There was just no one she would rather be with. Becca was her best friend, but no one could offer her the friendship her husband did. She was grateful for how much fun they had together, how they seemed to think the same thoughts at the same time, how they could love each other without saying a word. Yes, it was good to hear Robert share about this Trent Jefferson fellow he talked about so much, but she was glad the young man wasn't making their home a place where he felt free to hang out.

"Did he forget part of his gear again?"

Laughing as he bent over to untie his boots, he said, "No, I think I finally trained him better than that. Today was his turn to fix the meal. He was supposed to make chili for all the guys. Chief thought that would be a safe option for the kid. I mean, you brown the beef, throw in some spices and some cans of tomatoes and beans. How hard can it be? Well, let me tell you, I will never forget that first bite I put in my mouth. I shouldn't say first bite. It was the only bite. That whole pot of chili got thrown out."

"Go on, tell me. How did he mess it up? I can't imagine."

Grabbing his wife's hand to take her into the kitchen with him, Robert kept talking as he reached for a glass to fill with iced tea from their refrigerator, "You know how you put spices in, right? Well, those spices are in the spice rack over our stove at the station. They're all labeled and in alphabetical order, pretty much foolproof. Apparently, they aren't Trent-proof though. The kid put about half a cup of cinnamon in the chili. It was the weirdest thing I've ever eaten, especially when my mouth was watering for spicy chili."

"Poor guy. I'm guessing you're starved, huh?"

"For anything except chili. I don't think I'll be able to eat it for a long time. How about I grab a shower and take you out to eat? I could really go for a steak and baked potato about right now."

Agreeing to both the shower and the steak dinner, Kayleigh followed her husband upstairs to get ready for their night out. The way he made spontaneous decisions was one of the things she loved about him. She truly never had a dull moment as Mrs. Robert Wilson.

*

Trent threw his hat across the room, barely missing Gracie. When he saw how his golden retriever's tail dipped between her legs, his anger left him. Reaching down to pat the dog's ears, he whispered, "I'm sorry, Little Girl. I didn't mean to scare you."

As Gracie licked his hand, he knew he had been forgiven. If only he was as good with people as he was with animals. He couldn't remember a time when he hadn't been the awkward one. The kids in school had always been a mystery to him, and he still couldn't think about the pain he felt inside his own home. But animals had always seemed to understand him, and he had always loved them back.

Moving over to the couch, Trent patted the place beside him. Laughing as he saw the look Gracie gave him, he said, "Yeah, I know you're not allowed up here, but how about we make an exception tonight? I'd kind of like to have you near me."

Snuggling up to his dog who also was his best friend, Trent

thought back to his shift at work. He seemed to move two steps back for every step he moved forward. One thing he knew for sure, nothing was turning out the way he had planned. He wondered if it ever would.

Chapter Ten

Chief looked at his old friend from over the top of the icy cold bottle of Coke he was just starting to tip up to his mouth. He always could tell when something was bothering Robbie, even when no one else could. Glancing over at the chair where Kayleigh was relaxing and looking as happy as he had ever seen her, Chief knew his best friend's wife knew nothing of the struggle her husband was battling. Tonight wasn't the time to share any of that with her. Tonight was for sharing a meal with two of his favorite people, and leaving the past where it belonged, for the time being at least.

"You guys let me know when the steaks are ready, okay? The potatoes should be ready to come out of the oven in about ten minutes."

Hearing the lazy way his wife called out without even bothering to turn around, Robert smiled. He was sure she had no idea how much she meant to him. She was his reason for living, even though he had never told her how he felt in those exact words. He was afraid one innocent comment from him could lead to more questions from her than he would be comfortable answering. They had an amazing relationship, built on friendship and trust, and he didn't want to do anything to jeopardize their life together. Looking back toward the grill in time to see the look his friend flashed his way, Robert knew he had been caught. Neither man smiled. Both were thinking the same thing and neither wanted to acknowledge it, so they looked away briefly before returning to the banter they had been enjoying before Kayleigh had interrupted them.

It wasn't long before they had the food on the patio table and were seated together enjoying their meal. Kayleigh entertained them all with the never-ending drama that was her life at her office, comparing it to the sitcom they all often enjoyed watching together. Both men laughed as they assured her nothing exciting ever happened at the station. She had learned long ago that some of the things that happened at the fire station stayed there. She knew better than to ask them to share with her more than they were offering.

When Chief went home just after dark, Robert and Kayleigh cleared the patio table before going inside to finish up in the kitchen. Having long ago established a rhythm for this chore, both did their part quickly and were soon making their way to the den. Trading in their usual movie for a quiet night of reading, Robert settled down with a crime thriller he had just bought while Kayleigh snuggled up next to him with a stack of magazines.

When he heard the soft snoring he had grown to love so much over the years, he nudged his wife just a bit, waking her gently before saying, "Hey Babe, wake up. Let's go upstairs."

Loving the smile that crossed her face as she stood before allowing him to guide her up the stairs to their bedroom, he silently thanked God for her, just like he had done more times than he could count. He didn't deserve this woman, but he was grateful every day that she had come into his life.

*

Robert was glad he had an early shift the next morning. He had learned a long time ago to confront problems head-on and what had been going on at the station needed to be dealt with. He knew his friend was worried. Nothing like this had ever happened before. He knew it wouldn't take long before the relationships Chief had worked so hard to nurture among the men were ruined if something wasn't done. They both knew someone was stirring up trouble, but whoever was doing it was good at not getting caught. Robert had agreed to keep an eye out, maybe even stick his nose where it didn't normally belong, and hopefully find out who had been setting little traps around the station.

It had started out small, making everyone think they had a prankster on their hands. Pranks certainly weren't rare at a fire station. Laughing over antics during their downtime had quickly turned to annoyance. Running out of toilet paper repeatedly, listening to the voice of the person who yelled from the bathroom for someone to come help, seemed like a pathetic attempt at joking, but when tools started showing up out of place, the laughter suddenly stopped. What had been a bit of fun and games now felt more like a threat, and everything pointed to it being a threat from one of their own.

When Chief had approached him with his plan, Robert had agreed to come in early and stay late for a few weeks, maybe drive away sometimes only to walk back so he could hang around without being seen. He felt like one of the characters in the novels he loved to read so much, but unlike a mystery that was created from someone's imagination, what was going on at his job was all too real. And he agreed with Chief that things could get messy quickly.

*

Kayleigh looked up from her bowl of cereal when she heard keys at their front door. Knowing it was Robert made her smile, but she had a few things to ask him too.

"In here."

"Be there in a sec."

When he entered the kitchen a few seconds later, he took one look at his wife's face, quickly sitting down beside her before saying, "What's up? I've seen that look before."

Reaching over to take his hand in hers, Kayleigh let one

finger trace around his palm before looking up at him and asking, "You've not been yourself lately. I know something must be going on at work, and I understand if you can't discuss it with me. Really, I do. But I just wanted to make sure you know I'm here for you."

"It's okay. I caught a group of young boys, maybe twelve or thirteen years old, near the station this morning with some cans of spray paint. I scared them pretty good when I confronted them. They claimed they had no intention of doing anything to the station walls, but they also wouldn't fess up about why they had so much paint on them. I ended up letting them go, and I'm really hoping I don't end up regretting it."

"Well, they definitely didn't have anything good in mind, but maybe you scared them straight. It's kind of weird though. Why aren't kids that young at home? I mean I certainly never got up early on a Saturday to hang out with my friends like that."

"Nope. You slept in, didn't you?"

"Speaking of sleeping in, let's have a lazy day today. I have plenty I could work on, but I'm kind of thinking we could have a movie marathon on the couch."

Recognizing the gift his wife was offering, Robert hopped up and went with her to their den. Picking out three or four movies off their shelf for her to choose from, he joined her under the comfy blanket they kept on the back of their couch just for them. Yes, he was looking forward to spending the rest of the day at home. Maybe scaring those kids off this morning would solve his worries at work. No matter what, any thoughts of the station weren't welcome on this couch. Counting his blessings yet again, he snuggled up to the woman who had no idea how much he didn't deserve her.

Chapter Eleven

Fall 2015

Kayleigh hadn't had a dream in a few days and she was glad. As much as she loved her husband, she was starting to have moments that surprised her, moments where the grief didn't threaten to pull her under quite so much. These times made her feel guilty, but she had to admit they also were a welcome relief from what her life had been like since she had lost him. She needed some time just to be alone with herself. Some time to not think about the life she had shared with her husband and how much she was missing out on every single day.

Deciding to take advantage of her uncharacteristic good mood, she pulled out her phone and started tapping out a list. She had been thinking a lot lately about redecorating her home. If she was going to stay put, and deep in her heart she knew she had no intention of moving, then she needed to make it her space instead of keeping it the way it was now. Getting rid of Robert's clothes and the kitchen appliances he had used had been a great starting place, but she knew she needed to do an overhaul. She needed to make their home work for her now. She had always loved putting together giant jigsaw puzzles, so a puzzle table made it to her list. She had also always wanted a chaise lounge in their bedroom, but with their huge bed there just hadn't been room for one. She added one to her list now along with a smaller bed. Knowing she couldn't make all these changes in one day didn't dampen her spirits. Kayleigh grabbed her purse and keys as she headed out the door to make a dent in her list. She simply had to do something. After all, she needed to continue to move forward a little each day.

Texting Becca for lunch had been a good idea. Her friend wasn't free to drop everything and meet her at the mall like she had suggested, but she had, in typical best friend fashion, immediately included Kayleigh in the plans she had made with her family. Grateful and a little ashamed of herself, she thought back to the last time she had sent Becca a text. As she considered it, she was shocked to realize she couldn't remember reaching out to her since the funeral. Sure, her friend had made it a priority to come by for several visits, but it shamed her to realize she had failed to initiate a single correspondence before today. She knew Becca understood why, just like she knew she probably would never be the friend who sent silly memes and what she had called her text blessings ever again, but she was trying. And she knew that was all anyone expected of her. Besides, she was feeling like her old self today, and that was something she wanted to share with her best friend.

Driving up to Becca's house a few minutes later, she smiled as she saw the old van in the driveway. Mr. and Mrs. Jones had been driving it for as long as she had known them. They were wonderful people, and Kayleigh looked forward to seeing them every chance she got. They had both been supportive after Robert had died. Becca's dad had made the funeral arrangements while her mom had spent days cooking enough food to fill up Kayleigh's freezer. Neither were big talkers, and the gift of silence they offered her in the days following the accident had done so much to soften the blow of losing her husband. Just having them in the house with her, along with Becca, had helped keep her from drifting into a depression. They had anchored her, and she knew there would never be a way to repay them, so when Becca had invited her to have lunch with them all, she had abandoned her list and all thoughts of home improvement. She would choose canned soup and grilled cheese sandwiches with this family over her favorite place at the mall food court any day.

A few hours with Becca and her family left Kayleigh feeling more content than she had in a long time. Making up her mind to go shopping another day, she hugged them all before returning to her car for the drive back home. She was ready for whatever the rest of the day threw her way. Her new plan was to get caught up on housework and laundry before paying a few bills. Then she thought she might try one of the books Robert had kept on the shelf behind their couch. Never a huge fan of mysteries, she decided to see what it was about them that had made him buy one every time they went to the bookstore.

Later that evening, as she snuggled under a blanket in bed, she opened the thinnest book she had been able to find. Laughing at herself a little, she whispered, "Babe, I'm finally going to read one of those books you couldn't seem to put down. Let's see if this is one is as good as you always said they were."

After reading for an hour, Kayleigh looked at the clock, surprised at how much time had passed. She was also amazed at how quickly the story had hooked her. *Of course he was right. He was always right.* Even as she thought this, she had to smile. The book was good, and she knew she would be up a few more hours finishing it. She only wished she had her husband in bed beside her to tease her for not listening to him in the first place.

Chapter Twelve

Kayleigh couldn't remember ever waking up mad before. If Robert were still alive, she knew exactly what she would do. She would punch him in his shoulder until he woke up just so she could yell at him for what he had done in the dream. As a wave of realization washed over her, she felt her anger slowly melting away. Finally able to smile a little, she wished she could share with her late husband why he had made her so mad. Perhaps if she had him to talk to right now, she would be able to make some sense of it. She just didn't understand her anger though. Maybe it was because when she woke up, she honestly felt like she was still in the dream. The unsettling feeling stayed with her even after the anger had completely left.

"Becca? You free for lunch today?" Taking a few minutes before work to leave her best friend a voicemail made Kayleigh feel a little like her old self. She didn't have to think hard to imagine the smile that she knew would spread across her friend's face. They had just gotten together this weekend and she knew Becca would be thrilled to hear from her again so soon.

Hearing the soft sound from her phone hours later while at her desk made her smile. It had been a long time since her work had been interrupted by a text message. Even though she had to fight back a wave of sadness as the memories of long text conversations with Robert washed over her, she smiled as she read her friend's suggestion that they meet at their favorite sandwich shop. Typing back a quick reply, Kayleigh felt some of the heaviness lift from her shoulders. She was excited about having lunch with her friend, and she was surprised how good it felt to have something to look forward to again.

Walking into the restaurant thirty minutes later felt refreshingly normal too. Seeing the huge grin appear on her friend's face made Kayleigh's pace quicken. When she finally reached the table and bent down to give her a hug, she didn't want to let go. It felt good to feel someone's arms around her. Finally letting go, Kayleigh knew Becca pretended not to see when she wiped away the tears that were suddenly in her eyes.

She was that kind of friend.

"So, how excited was I to get a text from you about lunch again today? Girl, I've missed this, missed us. Don't get me wrong. Lunch with my folks was great, but I've missed having time alone with you."

Refusing to give in to the urge to duck her head, Kayleigh said, "I've missed you too. Thanks for everything you've done for me. There's just no way to express how much it meant. I know I haven't been there for you in the same way, but I'm feeling a little more like myself every day."

They quickly fell into their old rhythm of effortless banter. Kayleigh couldn't remember the last time she had smiled so much. Reaching across the table to give Becca's hand a quick squeeze, she noticed the waiter approaching their table. Quickly giving him their orders, Kayleigh smiled as she grabbed her friend's hand again. She had been waiting for him to walk away before bringing up the real reason she had asked her out to lunch today.

"Becca, you know how I told you about those dreams I've

been having?"

Nodding, Becca answered, "Yeah, of course I do. Are they still making you feel like Robert is with you?"

"More than you know. That's actually why I wanted to meet with you today." Picking up the white paper napkin left there by the waiter, Kayleigh began tearing it into tiny pieces before continuing, "Well, I had another one last night. This one was the most real of all. The weirdest thing about it was my reaction. Usually I wake up with this satisfied feeling that's hard to describe. It's like being with him, even if it's just in my dreams, is so real that I almost forget he's gone until I roll over and see his empty pillow. Did I tell you I finally washed it? It smelled like him for so long until one day it just didn't."

Giving Kayleigh a small sad smile, Becca waited to hear the rest. She had no idea what her friend's pain actually felt like, but she had figured out that it was usually best to just listen. So she waited patiently for her to continue.

"Here's the thing. This morning I was furious when I woke up. I think I would have lost it on Robert if he had been in bed with me. This dream was the most real one of all, and I didn't like my husband very much after I woke up. Oh my!" Throwing a hand up to cover her mouth, she whispered, "I'm a terrible person, aren't I?"

Reaching out to pull her friend's hand down from her face, Becca said, "You've been through so much, but trust me on this one thing. Kayleigh, you and Robert were perfect for each other. You aren't a terrible person at all. You were the best wife. Do you know how much I envied the two of you?" Continuing before she could respond, Becca added, "These dreams aren't real. I don't know why you're having them, but obviously it's your mind's way of dealing with everything. Whatever Robert did in the dream wasn't real."

"But Becca, it was so real to me. The way I felt when I woke up. I felt everything the girl in the dream did, and I hated Robert for what he did. I hated him."

"Do you want to tell me about the dream? You don't have to, but you know I'll listen."

The waiter picked that exact moment to arrive with their

salads and drinks. The pause was a welcome relief for Kayleigh. Yes, she needed to talk about this dream, but she was also a little worried about how she would handle it if the emotions from this morning flared up again. Explaining that she would tell her all about the dream after they ate, she shared the latest office gossip between bites of arugula, strawberries, and feta cheese.

Later, over dessert, she knew the time had come, so she pushed her plate with what was left of her cheesecake on it aside as she allowed the dream to pour itself out of her.

"Becca, everything was great. I was this young teenage girl who was obviously in love with Robert. He was wearing his high school basketball uniform, so it must have been after one of his games. In my dream, I was standing there talking to him before he went to the showers. I think we were talking about where we were going to go eat or something like that. I just know that I had this really settled feeling, like we were a solid couple. To be honest, I felt about him in the dream the way I feel about him now. I can't be sure, but if I had to guess I would say we were well past the just dating stage. That makes no sense because Robert always told me I was his first, and I honestly never had a reason to question that. But in the dream? I just knew that girl had been with him. Don't ask me how I know; I just know." Pausing to take a sip of her coffee, Kayleigh looked into Becca's eyes before picking up where she left off, "He was standing next to me one minute acting like the boyfriend he obviously was, and then the next minute he acted like he couldn't see me. It was like I had literally disappeared, but I hadn't. He just wasn't aware of me anymore at all because this other girl had walked up to us. The weird thing is she obviously walked up to me, not him. But it was like he had been waiting for her all along, like everything we had shared had been a set-up for that moment. Next thing I know, in the dream, we're all three in church on a pew together. The preacher called Robert out in front of everyone. From the pulpit! And he didn't even try to deny any of it. And that's when I woke up. Trust me, Becca, if you had tested my blood pressure this morning it would have been through the roof.

I've never been so mad."

"Kayleigh, do you have any idea who the other girl was?"

"No. I just know I knew her and trusted her. And I can't shake the feeling that Robert had wanted her all along. It was honestly like I had just been playing a part. I felt so used. And the worst part? I still loved him even while I hated him so much. I still feel that a little bit even now."

"I'm glad you told me, but I really don't know what to say. I don't think Robert would do something like that even as a teenager, so I can't imagine why your brain made all of that up."

"Is that what you think is happening? I know it sounds crazy, but do you think there's any chance he's actually reaching out to me?"

Seeing the way her friend's eyes teared up, Becca was careful to answer her softly as she said, "No. Honey, Robert's gone. These dreams are all you. I'm sorry. I know you want him to really be with you, but he's just not. Deep down inside you know it too."

Wiping her tears again as she reached to grab her purse from the floor, Kayleigh agreed, "I know he's not. It's just that these dreams feel so real. Thanks for listening though. And thanks for helping me put it all into perspective." Hugging her as they walked away from the table, she added, "I need to get back to work now."

Putting her arm around her friend as they left the restaurant, Becca paused on the sidewalk and said, "I know this one thing. Robert Wilson adored you from the minute he laid eyes on you. I don't know about his past just like I don't know about these dreams, but for more than twenty years he was all yours. Keep that in your heart if you have another one of these bad dreams, okay?"

Hugging Becca again before saying good-bye, Kayleigh wished she could believe her words. While it was true she had always believed she and her husband had enjoyed a near-perfect relationship while he was alive, she couldn't shake this persistent feeling that she really hadn't known him at all.

Chapter Thirteen

April 2015

Trent wished he didn't make so many stupid mistakes. He tried to keep up with everything Robert tried to teach him, but he just couldn't. And he kept making them, mistakes that could cost someone their life one day. Maybe even his own.

Storing his gear in his locker, he slammed the door with enough force to make it fly back open, barely missing his face. Reaching up to close it softer this time, he turned and saw Robert standing behind him.

"What's got you so fired up tonight?"

Not wanting to offend the older man, Trent replied with, "It's nothing."

Grunting instead of saying what he wanted to, Robert brushed past the firefighter whose purpose in life seemed to be to annoy him. And things had been going so well, right up until they weren't. He wished he knew why the kid seemed to struggle some days more than others. Lately it seemed like

Trent Jefferson was messing up more things than he was getting right. He could only hope it was a serious case of the jitters. Chief had trusted him to help bring this man who acted more like a boy into the family and he wouldn't stop trying to do that, but he knew the morale of the entire fire station depended on it. He decided to reach out yet again.

"Wait up, Trent. I was just about to grab a bite to eat. Care to join me?"

Smiling his first real smile in at least a few days, Trent responded with, "Sure. Let me grab a quick shower first. Meet you somewhere?"

After making plans to meet in thirty minutes at a burger joint down the road, Robert left feeling lighter than he had in some time. Maybe he would be able to talk to him, get inside his head a bit. He couldn't remember ever seeing a firefighter struggle so much with the basics. Maybe something else was going on, something he could help Trent with. One thing was certain, something had to be done fast. He didn't know if he had the patience to deal with all of this much longer.

*

Kayleigh smiled as she read her husband's text. Of course he was ditching her in order to take some young guy out for a burger. She loved her husband for doing things like that. He was the kindest person she knew and if he was bailing on her to go eat dinner with someone else, then she knew whoever he was helping must really need it. How could she let it upset her?

Spooning out a bowlful of the goulash she had thrown together quickly as soon as she had gotten home from work, she decided to take it into their den to eat. Not a fan of much that was on television, she decided on a game show. She loved watching them even though she rarely got many of the questions right. It was a running joke between her and Robert. Neither of them would make a penny if they ever managed to pass whatever test you had to take to audition for one of those shows, but they sure had fun watching them.

When she heard Robert drive up a couple of hours later, she had watched at least four different game shows. She couldn't wait to tell him her scores. He would get a kick out of how few questions she had gotten right.

"Babe, I'm home."

"I'm in here watching television."

As Robert peeked his head around the corner to stare at his lovely wife, he asked, "Game shows?"

"You know it. I maybe knew half a dozen answers out of the hundred or so they asked. Man, I'm so bad at these."

Bending down to give her a kiss on her forehead, he softly said, "But you look so good. Seriously. Kayleigh, I don't tell you enough. You're gorgeous."

Smiling up at him, loving how close his face was to hers, she simply said, "Thank you." She knew he would hear, in his heart, all the words she hadn't said. It had always been that way with them. They truly were one, and she made a point of thanking God every day for the gift that her husband was to her.

As Robert sat down beside her, he shared the conversation from earlier, telling her how concerned he was for the young man. As she offered words of encouragement, all he could do was smile back at her. How had he gotten so blessed to have this amazing woman in his life?

Later, as they made their way upstairs to the bed they shared, Kayleigh put her arm around his waist as she told him, "Don't be so hard on yourself. You can only help people if they want to be helped. I agree that this kid is struggling to find his place at the station, but do you think he might just be immature? I don't know as much as you do, of course, but it may not be as serious as you think."

"You might be right. Here's the deal though. When we get to the top of the stairs, no more work talk, okay? I shouldn't have even brought it home with me."

Pretending to break into a jog to get to the top faster, Kayleigh giggled as she whispered, "Deal."

Chapter Fourteen

March 2016

Becca woke up and stared at the ceiling for a few minutes. She was worried about her best friend, but she didn't know what to do about it. Robert had been gone for almost a year, and Kayleigh was still going on and on about her dreams. At first, she had thought they were a good thing. She knew everyone dealt with shock differently, so, in the beginning, she had smiled encouragingly, trying to console her friend. But as the months passed, the dreams became more and more disturbing. And Kayleigh seemed to be losing her grip on reality. Becca was at a loss, so she reached out to the only person she trusted to keep all this a secret.

Calling her mom a few minutes later, she unloaded everything that had been bothering her since Robert had died that day in the hospital. Loving her mom for the silence she heard on the other end, she knew as soon as she paused to take a breath she would be offered the words of wisdom she desperately needed to hear.

"Sorry, Mom. I know I probably overshared, but I'm in over my head here. I'm seriously worried about Kayleigh. Do you think I should be?"

"Well, I know we all grieve differently. And I also know our minds can play tricks on us. But, Honey, you have to consider another possibility."

When her mother didn't immediately continue, Becca had to control herself. She knew her mom, and she knew whatever she was thinking right now would eventually be turned into words. Helpful words. Words that Kayleigh probably needed to hear too. So she waited.

"Becca, you don't know everything about Robert and Kayleigh like you think you do. There may be a reason she's having these dreams that has nothing to do with his death. Have you ever considered that she might be trying to work through more than just the accident?"

"What do you mean? You know as well as I do that if anyone had a perfect marriage it was those two. I've never seen two people more in love, and to hear her tell it, they never even had a fight."

"Hmmm…in two decades of marriage? No fighting? What about all those years they dated in college? Oh Becca, trust me. They fought. I'd like to think your dad and I have a great marriage too, but we certainly fight. A lot. I think all couples do."

With a laugh that had more than a twinge of bitterness hiding underneath it, Becca softly responded, "I wouldn't know. I can't remember the last time I was the other half of a couple."

"All in God's timing, my dear. Now back to Kayleigh. I don't know why she's having these dreams, but I don't think there's a real reason for you to be worried. She's a smart girl. She knows Robert's gone, and she knows deep down that he's not speaking to her through these dreams. Not really anyway. My guess is she's processing the past twenty-five years of her life. I think the grief, and the sudden way it appeared, has brought a lot to the surface. Probably more than she can handle. Maybe her mind is releasing a little bit of her past at a time, letting her deal with it by dreaming. I think they are actually made up of bits and pieces of conversations she had over the years with Robert, forgotten memories of pictures she's seen, and probably even just feelings she had throughout their relationship. I doubt she has any true memories of any of it, but I think what's been buried deep inside of her is coming to the surface. To be honest, I think it's a good thing. Just like I think you're a good friend for caring so much about her."

Wiping the tears away that had been falling for the past several minutes as she listened to her mom's soothing voice, the one she remembered so well from her childhood, Becca thanked her before ending the call. She had a lot to think about. Somehow the wisdom her mom had just effortlessly poured out needed to be transferred to Kayleigh. Becca knew she needed time to process her mom's wisdom, and she hoped she could remember it all. One thing was for sure. She needed to pay her best friend a visit. If she had been questioning her friend's coping skills, she could only imagine the anguish

Kayleigh had been going through.

Chapter Fifteen

April 2015

Kayleigh had to laugh at her husband's frustration. He had coached more basketball teams over the years than she could possibly count, she knew he had experienced his share of immature players, so why was this one young firefighter causing him so much grief? She cared about his feelings, but she also seriously wanted to tease him. Who knew her husband was so adorably cute when things didn't go his way?

"Kayleigh, I almost don't want to go in today. Usually I'm totally psyched for my shift, but knowing Trent Jefferson is waiting at the station almost makes me want to call Chief and tell him I can't make it."

Resisting the smile that was struggling to not find its way to her face, she settled for a somber look as she told him, "You can handle anything anyone dishes out. Robert, I've never known anyone like you. You're the kindest person on the planet. Don't you know everyone feels better after just being around you?"

Squeezing his hands into fists, he answered, "I'm not all that you think I am."

Not hearing the subtle warning under his words, Kayleigh allowed her face to break into a smile as she told him, "Actually you're all that and a bag of chips."

*

April 2016

Kayleigh wasn't sure what made that particular memory come to her mind today. It seemed Robert was visiting her in her memories during the day now as much as he was showing up at night in her dreams. Somehow this memory was more real than the conversation had been when they had looked into each other's eyes as they stood in their kitchen together that morning so long ago. It felt like a lifetime had passed, but the memory brought it all back and into focus for her.

What had Robert been hinting at? She wished she had been just a little wiser back then. Maybe if she had paused before teasing him, he would have explained what it was about himself that she didn't know. She sure would give anything to hear his answer now.

But, no, her love had blinded her to whatever he had been trying to tell her. She suddenly was overcome with shame as she considered how she had robbed her husband that day. Looking back, she could clearly see that there was something he had wanted to get off his chest, a burden he had wanted to share with her. How many other times had she failed to be the wife he needed? The realization brought instant tears to her eyes as she cried out to her husband even though she knew he would never again be able to hear her words, "Oh Robert, I'm so sorry. If I had the chance to do it all over again, I promise I would listen more carefully this time. I'd give anything for the chance to hold you and tell you I love you no matter what."

Unable to even consider what he had meant by his mysterious comment that day, Kayleigh made her way up the stairs to the one room in the house she hadn't changed since her husband's death. Every other corner of their home had a fresh look, designed to help her move forward, but not this room. Not this sanctuary, this place where she had loved her husband in the way no one else ever could. No, this was one room that still belonged to the two of them. It was the only place she seemed to really feel him anymore, even if it was in her dreams.

*

She woke up with an unbearable urge to touch Robert. Raising her fisted hands to her eyes, she fought the urge to scream. Feeling like a child, one too young to understand why she was being denied the simple act of human touch, Kayleigh sat up, asking God again, as she had so many times over the past months, why? Why had her husband died? Why was she being equally comforted and tormented by these dreams? And why had she been given such an incredible love only to be left with nothing? She was alone, and she hated it. The worst part was how she was so confused about it all.

Throwing her covers off quickly, Kayleigh got out of bed even though she knew her alarm wasn't set to go off for at least two more hours. She knew, after that dream, there was no more sleep to be had for her.

Making her way downstairs, she quickly fixed herself a cup of tea before heading to the couch. After wrapping up in the blanket that was noticeably too big for one person, she sipped her drink and stared at the soft light trying to creep in through the small crack at the bottom of the blinds. Robert had always teased her that someone was peeking in even though the space between the end of the blinds and the windowsill was almost too thin to slip a piece of paper through. She sighed as she thought about how memories of her husband were everywhere in their home. And how memories just weren't enough.

Allowing her mind to drift back to the dream that had ended any chance of more sleep for her, Kayleigh was surprised when she realized the Robert in this dream was one she had actually known. As she put all the pieces of the dream together before her brain blurred them into something unrecognizable, she realized the time frame of this one would have been just a couple of years ago. It made no sense to her that her dreams would shift forward so much in time. She and Robert had spent every waking moment together when he wasn't working his grueling twenty-four hour shifts or some of the occasional part-time hours he picked up, not for the money anymore so much as to help one of the other men out of a tight spot. Her work hours were fairly regular, and on his days off they spent their evenings together. He had spent a lot of time helping his parents before they had died, a blessing she had been proud of as much as the way he took such good care of their own home and yard during the day on his time off when she was at work. Even though she pitched in, especially when he was at work, she had always known what a gift it was to have a husband who enjoyed shopping for groceries and preparing wonderful meals. They had made a great team, and it had never once crossed her mind that there were any secrets between them until she had started having these dreams. Before tonight, even the dreams seemed to be something her imagination had worked up. She hadn't asked for expert advice, but she also was fairly certain dreaming was a natural part of the grieving process. And she knew the key was to process it over time because she couldn't imagine her grief ever truly ending.

Tonight's dream caused her world to come crashing down a bit. Just like she had before in all the other ones, she had been with Robert. In fact, they had been at a local coffee shop they both loved. The key difference between this dream and all the times she had enjoyed a cup of tea while watching her husband pour an unhealthy amount of sugar in the cup of coffee he seemed to truly enjoy ruining was who was watching him stir it with the little wooden stick. As she watched him, feeling a smile on her lips, she felt a strong sense of dread settling into her stomach. Being there, in that chair across from her husband, almost knocked her to the floor. Why would Robert meet another woman for coffee? And who was she? As the dream had gone on, Kayleigh had the nagging feeling that the two had known each other for a long time. There was something familiar about the way they sat together and talked, even though she didn't miss the subtle signs of discomfort radiating from her husband. As he made small talk in that casual way he had that always put other people at ease, she could tell he was afraid of this woman. None of it had made sense in the dream, and now, as she allowed the blanket and tea to warm her, she still didn't understand. As she got to the bottom of her cup, she stared at the window, at the small sliver of light that was much brighter than it had been just a few minutes earlier. Another light was dawning too. This one was on the inside of her and its brightness brought a coldness with it that she knew no amount of blankets or tea would take away. Her husband had kept secrets from her. And one of his secrets involved another woman. What else didn't she know?

Chapter Sixteen

April 2015

Robert purposely stayed in the shower longer than necessary. Pushing his hand against the wall above him as he allowed his head to rest in the crook of his arm, he wished he had answers to all the questions swirling around inside of him right now. What would happen if he stepped out from under the water and found Kayleigh? How would she react if he opened up and told her everything? Allowing the water to once again spray over his face, he washed away all thoughts of telling his wife the one secret he kept from her, the one truth about himself that he feared would be all it would take to cause their world together to come crashing down. He struggled to love himself, had for all these years, and he couldn't imagine his wife would be able to still love him if she knew the ugliness that lurked inside of him. No, he had been right to keep it a secret for all these years. Only one other person knew everything, but he trusted him with his life. Chief was so much more than his best friend; what had happened years ago had forged a bond between the two that made them more like brothers than any two men who shared the same parents. He just wished his wife didn't build him up so much. If she only knew he wasn't even a fraction of the man she thought he was.

*

April 2016

Chief knew he should be doing more than he was. Robbie would expect him to take care of Kayleigh. Even though the two men had never sat down and had an actual conversation about any of it, they both had always known the dangers involved with their job. Just like they both knew the other would step up if it was ever needed. The guilt was slowly eating away at him, but he just couldn't stand the look in his best friend's wife's eyes. She was pitiful. Seeing the intense love for his closest friend in the world clearly reflected in her eyes every time she looked at him made him feel like such a traitor. He knew things that would cause her to question the past quarter century of her life. Things he wished he could erase from his own memory. But time had a way of amplifying the past, and he found himself often staring at nothing at all while clearly seeing everything that had gone so unbelievably wrong that night long ago.

Yes, he should be stopping by to see if his best friend's wife needed anything. He should be showing up on Saturday mornings to mow her lawn. She should know to call him if she needed a plumber or an electrician or help with any of the other odd jobs Robbie had taken care of. But he hadn't made that offer, and she hadn't asked for anything from him. Every day he felt like he was letting his friend down just a little bit more. The heaviness of it all weighed on him, and he just didn't know what to do to lighten the load.

He couldn't help but think back to that night and all it had brought with it.

*

May 1991

"I can't believe she's dead."

"Robbie, you gotta pull yourself together. Man, this is too

much. Do you think it was an accident? Tell me you think it was an accident."

"Mark, this was no accident. You heard what her family's been saying. There was a witness who saw the whole thing. She eased across the center line and just kept driving. Man, how did she do that? She hit that truck head on. I can't…I just can't deal with any of this."

"Look. No one knows about what went down between the two of you. And no one really knows what happened that night either. Maybe her car had something wrong with it."

Running his hand through his hair before softly hitting the top of his head with his fist, Robbie said, "Let's go. I need to get home. Somehow I have to go to her funeral and face her family. I wonder if any of them know. Do you think any of them know?"

"I have no clue. I hate to even ask this, but do you think you should tell her parents? I mean, she obviously was very upset; maybe that's why she wasn't paying attention. Does anyone even know you were the last person to see her?"

Robbie turned his wild eyes toward his best friend as he answered, "No. No one knows anything. I mean she had just told me. I can't believe how mad I got at her. I think she was more afraid of me than she was sad about what Meghan had done, and she was devastated. She told me I was the biggest mistake of her life, and then she got in her car and drove away. She was crying pretty bad. Do you think she couldn't see? Oh man, do you think she didn't even know she was driving in the wrong lane?"

"You're asking questions none of us will ever know. Listen to me, okay? You have a decision to make. Do you let her carry your secret to her grave or not? It's that simple. Think about it. What good will it do anyone if you tell the truth now? It's only going to cause her family more pain. Man, I can't tell you what to do, but you need to look at the big picture here. Don't let distraction get a foothold. It's only gonna cause you regret in the long run. And it will just be one more thing to keep her mom up at night crying. And her dad will probably kill you. We both know no one else is going to want to talk about it either, especially Meghan. I think you just need to let it all go."

"Don't you think I've thought about all that already? But how do I go to that funeral and look any of them in the eye? How do I look at my parents ever again? I wish I never laid eyes on her. Either of them."

Mark couldn't stand seeing Robbie this way. They had been friends since they met as snaggle-toothed first graders, and they had shared everything with each other since. As far as he knew, they hadn't ever kept secrets from each other, but now he wasn't so sure his friend was telling him the truth.

"Robbie, what really happened between you two? Some of the stuff you just said doesn't make sense to me. I don't want to get in your business, but if there's anything you want to talk about, you know I'm here for you, right?"

Looking his friend in the eye for the first time in a while, Robbie decided it was time to open up. Mark was right about one thing; this was a story he needed to get off his chest, and if he couldn't trust his best friend, then who could he trust?

"Okay." Taking a deep breath, he continued, "Mark, I'm

just gonna tell you the whole story like it happened. Maybe you can help me make sense out of it. I just can't understand how things got so out of control, and I sure don't know how she's dead now. Anyway, here goes."

As the story poured out of his friend, Mark had to bite the inside of his cheek several times to keep from interrupting. This was Robbie's story to tell, no matter how hard it was to hear.

Chapter Seventeen

March 1991

"Sarah, it's not what you're thinking. I'm sorry. Robbie and I didn't want to fall in love. It just happened."

Sarah couldn't even look at her sister. Robbie Wilson had acted like he loved her, but obviously it was only a trick to get what he really wanted. And now her sister truly believed he was in love with her. How could she explain to Meghan that guys like Robbie were only after one thing? She should know. Just like she knew that no matter what she said right now, she would sound like the jealous jilted lover she was. But she loved Meghan too much not to tell her, especially since all of this was her fault.

"Meghan, I'm definitely mad at him. And I'd be lying if I didn't admit I'm a little mad at you too, but I'm also mad at myself. I was furious at you that night in the gym and for quite a few weeks afterwards. I gotta tell you something though. I've had time to really think about everything, and I figured something out, something you need to hear. Will you listen? Please?"

Unable to resist the tenderness she heard in her older sister's voice, Meghan nodded without lifting her gaze from the floor she had been staring at since this conversation had started.

"Thanks, Meg. Okay, here goes. I was blind to who Robbie really was, is. I was so happy a senior was interested in me; I just didn't see the signs. Now I can see how he was setting me up all along. You see, it was you he wanted, but that didn't stop him from using me first. Meghan, you're too young for what he wants. Trust me on this. You need to break up with him."

Looking up, Meghan met her sister's eyes for the first time all night as she said, "Sarah, you just don't get it. We're in love. Robbie told me he thought he was in love with you until he spent time with me. He said something came over him, and he just had to have me. I'm really sorry. I am. But, Sarah, can't you be happy for us? I'm sorry about what happened to you, but isn't that the most romantic thing ever? He was happy enough to date you, but he said that seeing me made him realize what true love really is."

Shaking her head, Sarah simply said, "You're making such a mistake. I won't tell Mom and Dad, but please make me this one promise. Don't spend time alone with him."

Giggling like the little girl she was, Meghan said, "Why not? Spending time alone with him is where all the fun is at. And he has a truck! We can go anywhere we want."

"Yeah, but you don't really understand what that means. That truck also means he can do anything he wants."

"You worry too much. Look, let's just not talk about him anymore. I don't want what I have with him to come between us."

Reaching up to give her little sister a hug, Sarah lifted off the bed before giving her an answer, "Okay, but I still don't approve. And even though I realize now what a huge mistake he was, I'd be lying if I didn't tell you that it all still hurts."

*

April 1991

"Do you remember that note you wrote me? The one I keep beside my bed?"

Smiling up at him as he asked her this, Meghan tossed her ponytail over her shoulder as she answered, "Of course. I think about that note all the time. Why?"

When Robbie looked at her this time, she stopped smiling. She couldn't quite put her finger on it, but there was something different about the energy between them. Suddenly, she felt an overwhelming urge to run away even though she knew that was completely irrational. One thing was certain, all the joy she had felt when he had first mentioned the love note she had written to him was gone. In its place was an uneasiness she found very uncomfortable. That feeling shifted quickly as she listened to his next words.

"Well, I burned it. Look, I know we both used to feel that way, but I just don't anymore. I'm sorry I let this go this far."

Unable to speak, she just stared at him.

"You understand, right?" Robbie couldn't quite look her in the eye as he added, "I guess you need to go now."

At this obvious dismissal, Meghan doubled over, feeling a pain as real as if he had stabbed her with a knife. Her tears were instant and uncontrollable. It scared her how quickly they turned into deep sobs. She didn't fight the urge to run this time, leaving Robbie behind as she ran to her bike and pedaled as far away from him as possible. She had been such a fool. And she alone was to blame for all she had lost.

The pain stayed with her for weeks. It was unrelenting. And she had absolutely no one to share it with because she had allowed her blind love for Robbie to cost her the relationship with her favorite person, the person she had treasured her entire life. If only she hadn't been so focused on him. If only she hadn't been so proud when he chose her.

*

May 1991

"So you dumped Sarah? I don't get it. You barely dated her."

"No, not Sarah."

"Wait. I don't get it. Robbie, I don't remember you dating anyone else. Who is the girl in your story?"

"Mark, there's so much more to the story. I dated Meghan after Sarah and I split up. But she was just too young, so I convinced her that we needed to keep it all a secret. We dated for about six months and no one knew. We kept everything a secret. And I do mean everything."

"Man, I don't get what this has to do with Sarah's accident. Why would it matter that you dated her kid sister? Even if that is pretty messed up. Why would you dump a pretty girl like Sarah and go after her little sister? Isn't she in middle school?"

"I'm not proud of what I did. And I did a lot more than you know."

"So, tell me the rest." Mark tried hard not to sound like he was judging Robbie, but he just couldn't figure out why his best friend would mess with a girl so young.

*

May 1991

Sarah couldn't stand what she was seeing. Her sister was miserable at home, and even though he acted like he didn't care, she couldn't help but believe Robbie at least felt a little bad about the break-up too. Watching him at school certainly made her suspect that he was eaten up with guilt about the way he had treated both of them. Even though she had dated him first, she was torn, like she was in the middle of it all, watching the two of them without being able to offer either one the help she knew they both needed. She didn't want them to get back together. It wasn't because she wanted Robbie Wilson; she was beyond over him. She just hated to see her sister in such agony, and if Robbie felt even a fraction of what Meghan did, then he was hurting too.

Knowing that she could help heal them, and not having the freedom to share what she saw with either one, was almost more than she could hold inside her heart. Why had she seen that look on his face? Why had she been entrusted with his pain, even if he had not meant to share it with her? She would give anything to help them, but her hands were tied, so she sat by and watched them both suffer. She knew her little sister enough to know there was more to the story, but she didn't want to pry. Meghan would tell her when she was ready. And even though part of her hated Robbie, she couldn't help but feel sorry for him too. In a way, she felt like all of this was her fault. After all, if she hadn't given him her phone number, then Meghan never would have met him. She wasn't sure she'd ever be able to forgive herself. In fact, she was sure it would be easier to forgive Robbie for the way he had used her. He was just a dumb boy after all, but she was supposed to protect her little sister, not lead her to the person who had obviously broken her heart. She knew what she had to do and dreaded it. Just the thought of talking to Robbie again made her skin crawl, but she knew she had to confront him. And the sooner she did, the sooner she could put this all behind her. She could only hope Meghan could get Robbie off her mind too. She wanted her sister back, no matter what it cost her.

*

May 1991

Mark couldn't believe what he was hearing. How could his best friend go out with a little kid? It made him sick to think about where this story was going, but he had to ask, "So, tell me one thing. Did you just hang out with Meghan or did y'all really date?"

Robbie couldn't stop the blush that covered his face no

matter how much he hated for his best friend to see it. Realizing his red face was all the answer Mark would ever need, he simply shook his head instead of answering.

Mark said, "I see. So did Sarah find out? Is that why she was so upset? What? She caught you with her little sister or something?"

"I wish it was something that simple. Look, there's more I need to tell you. I know what you must be thinking about me right now, but trust me when I say it's nothing like you're gonna be thinking when you hear the rest. It gets worse."

*

April 1991

Sarah didn't like the way her sister was looking lately. She could tell something was wrong, but Meghan had made it very clear that she didn't want to talk to her, about anything, certainly not about Robbie. But she had to know what was going on, so she knocked softly on her bedroom door before opening it just a crack as she called out, "Okay if I come in?"

Hearing a small sound from inside the dark room was all the encouragement she needed. As she went in, making her way to the bed where she knew Meghan would be, she sat down, content to wait until her sister wanted to tell her what was going on. She knew it involved Robbie, just like she knew she'd give anything to go back in time to the day he had made her feel so special by asking for her number. If only she had known the trouble he would cause. She wished more than anything that she had never met the boy.

"Oh Sarah, I've done something really bad."

Hearing the way her sister's voice sounded made her want to crawl under the covers and hold her. But she knew Meghan better than anyone, knew that she needed her space right now. She hoped her sister didn't feel as bad as she sounded, but something told her it was worse than she could imagine.

"You can tell me anything, you know?"

"Sarah? Promise me you won't hate me?"

"Meg, you know better than that. Remember that time you took my favorite Barbie to school and traded it with some girl? What did you trade it for? It seems like it was for some baseball cards or something really dumb. Let me tell you, I was so mad, but even then I didn't hate you. Don't you know I could never hate you?"

With tears streaming down her face, Meghan sat up and leaned into her sister, finally giving Sarah the chance to hug her. After a few minutes, Meghan said, "He dumped me. I had news to share with him, but before I could even open my mouth to tell him, he blew me off. Acted like I never meant anything to him at all. After he broke up with me, I just left. I got on my bike and rode away as fast as I could. I was so upset, but I didn't think I could tell you all about it because I hadn't told you about the other."

Stroking her sister's hair in the way she used to do when they were much younger, Sarah gently asked, "The other?"

With a voice that was barely above a whisper, Meghan said the two words that seemed to suck all the air out of the room, "The baby."

Dropping to her knees and spinning around to grab Meghan's hands, Sarah asked, "You're pregnant?"

When Meghan just shook her head, it took a minute for Sarah to figure it all out, but when she did, she let out a moan before saying, "Oh no, Meghan." even though she knew what her sister had done. How many girls at school had told her about how they were able to make their problems go away? How many times had she wondered how they could possibly go through with it? But, if she were being honest with herself, she hadn't really cared about them. She had felt like she was better than they were because she knew she would never allow herself to get in the same kind of trouble. And now her baby sister was one of them, and it was her job to take care of her, to pick up all the broken pieces. As if all of that didn't hurt enough, she had to admit that Robbie had wanted her sister more than he had wanted her. As much as he sickened her right now, the rejection still hurt. And, unlike her sister, she had no one to share her pain with.

*

May 1991

"Wait. You got her pregnant? How could you be so dumb?"

Unable to get mad at his best friend for speaking the truth, Robbie answered, "Oh, I was dumb all right. She never told me though. I broke up with her, and she never even told me she was gonna have a baby. Sarah's actually the way I found out about the abortion. Well, she didn't tell me. I guess you could say she confronted me. I've never seen anyone so mad."

Mark was having trouble putting all the pieces together so he asked, "When did Sarah confront you?"

"Last week."

"Wow, so that's why she came to see you? I gotta ask this. When did Meghan have the abortion? I mean, I don't know the girl, but it seems like if she was walking around pregnant all this time someone would have noticed."

"I don't know. According to Sarah, Meghan didn't share the details with her. I don't get why she didn't tell me she was pregnant though. Sarah acted like she'd been listening to Meghan cry every night. I guess some girls don't get over abortions or something."

Wondering if his best friend was cold or just stupid or maybe a little bit of both, Mark said, "Well, she's awfully young. I don't know much about what they do, but it's like a medical thing, right? It probably hurt her. And, let's face it, you broke her heart."

"I still don't get why Sarah ran into that truck though. I mean Meghan's the one whose been so upset, right? Why did Sarah die?"

Mark didn't know what to say, so he just shook his head.

Robbie wasn't feeling like talking anymore, so he said, "Let's keep this between us, okay? One thing's for sure. I don't ever want to hear anything about Meghan again. I'm just so glad I'll be at college when she gets in high school. I don't think I could handle passing her in the hall every day."

Reaching out to pull his friend into a hug, Mark answered, "Your secret's safe with me." And he meant it.

Chapter Eighteen

April 2016

Kayleigh woke up with a dull pain in her chest. Looking up at the ceiling, she took a quick assessment of her body. Once she was certain there was nothing physically wrong with her, she let her eyes close, allowing herself to slip back into her dream just enough to remember what she knew she should want to forget.

The pain she had felt in her dream when Robert had told her he burned the note was almost as bad as the pain she had felt when she said good-bye to him in the hospital. Who was this girl? How was Robert that close to someone, close enough to cause her this kind of pain? She couldn't deny that what she was feeling now came from more than what the girl in the dream had felt. Knowing her husband had kept it all from her was the hardest part to understand. She had spent the past twenty years thinking there were no secrets between them, but she knew better now. There had been enough dreams to convince her that there were secrets about her husband she needed to know. If only she knew how the dreams were speaking to her. The only thing that made sense was what Becca had told her. Her grief must be causing memories she didn't know she had made to come to the surface. Whatever was going on, it no longer left her with the strange sense of comfort she had felt when they had first started. Now she almost had a desire to snoop around to see what other secrets Robert had kept from her. But where would she start? She had already cleaned out the entire house except their bedroom, getting rid of a lot of stuff that forced her to remember her husband. And what little was left consisted of items she had looked at many times since he had died. No, Robert had not left behind any secret journals or pictures or anything else that would help her find the answers to the questions that were adding up in her mind more and more every day.

Kayleigh found herself wishing for a mother for the first time in a long time. This made her think about Robert's mom. She would be such a comfort right now. And maybe she would be able to unravel the mystery of this girl who obviously had once upon a time had her heart broken by a boy she never knew, a man she thought she had known completely.

*

Chief hated to show up unannounced, but he knew it wouldn't take much to talk him out of this much overdue visit to his best friend's widow. He was sure, by now, that she would have a few chores that needed to be done around the house. Kayleigh was a strong woman, but there were bound to be things she couldn't handle on her own. Things that Robbie would have easily taken care of if he were still here. No, he shouldn't have driven over here without calling first, but he knew it wouldn't take long for Kayleigh to recover from the shock and accept his help.

Walking up to the familiar front porch, the first thing he noticed was how nice everything looked. There were new flowers in the monogrammed planters that had been part of Kayleigh's signature style as long as he had known her. It made him smile to see them. They were a welcome sign that she was getting out, trying to find ways to bring beauty to her world, and maybe even moving on a bit. As much as he hated to wish for it, he hoped she would find someone else to love. A woman like Kayleigh Wilson, so young and full of life, shouldn't be alone for the rest of her life. But that wasn't why he had come by today, so he reeled those thoughts in as he reached out to ring her doorbell.

As the door opened, Chief let his eyes focus on the sight before him for a beat before he spoke. Kayleigh had obviously been in the middle of something and, judging by the apron she wore and the towel she was using to wipe her hands, it had involved something in the kitchen. The thin line of flour on her forehead made him smile. He remembered that look. The woman could bake the best chocolate chip cookies he had ever tasted, but she absolutely destroyed the kitchen in the process.

"Chief, so good to see you. Did you smell the cookies all the way at the station and decide to come sample a few?"

Liking the smile he heard in her voice, he decided to play along as he answered her with, "You know it. I hope you have a couple dozen ready to come out of the oven right now. I haven't had any of your famous cookies in a long time."

"Come on in. I don't want them to burn."

Following her into the sunny kitchen he had helped Robbie paint a bright yellow color so many years ago, Chief fought hard to keep the memories from overwhelming him. Today wasn't about bringing any of his sadness over the death of his best friend into Kayleigh's life. No, this was a day to try and lighten her load. From what he could see as he followed her into the kitchen, she had things under control. He could tell she had changed the house quite a bit too, and although it was a bit of a shock, he understood. She had to create her own life, one without Robbie, now that she was alone. And judging by the new furniture he could see, she had chosen a lighter, more feminine look for the place.

"Yum! It smells good in here. You sure you have some to spare?"

Laughing at the man she considered to be more like family than just a friend, Kayleigh handed him a plate and told him to go sit at the table. Pulling out a pair of light blue potholders, she quickly had the cookie sheet out of the oven and on the wire rack that he assumed was used to help the cookies cool. Glad when he saw her grab a spatula, he felt his mouth water in anticipation of the treat he knew would soon be in his mouth. He wasn't sure how she did it, and he certainly would never ask for the recipe, but the taste of butter in the cookies made him want to eat more than was safe for his waistline. But today wasn't a day to worry about that. No, today he planned to eat his fill, talk to his friend's wife, and then hopefully do whatever he could to make her life a little easier.

Hours later, after he had put together a bookcase in Kayleigh's new office, fixed a leaky faucet in the kitchen, and installed a new shower head in the upstairs bathroom, he made his way outside to the backyard where she had told him she would be. Watching her working in the flower garden he had always admired, Chief thought about how proud Robbie would be right now. Kayleigh was doing okay. He hadn't missed the look of sadness that had entered her eyes a couple of times as they had chatted over the cookies earlier, but she had held her own. He knew that was all Robbie would have expected of her. He also knew his friend would be grateful for the work he had done today. He made a vow to himself to not let as much time go by before he paid her another visit.

"Kayleigh? I'm heading out unless you need something else."

Standing up while wiping the dirt from her hands, she smiled at him from under the ridiculously huge straw hat she was obviously wearing to avoid the sun. Walking toward him, she reached out her arms for a hug as she said, "How can I thank you? Those chores were probably a piece of cake for you, but I just didn't know how I was going to take care of them without hiring someone."

"You will do no such thing." Pulling out of the hug, Chief looked her in the eyes as he added, "If you ever need anything, you call me, hear? Don't ever hire anyone. Well, I'm not saying I'll do it for free though. I expect cookies as payments."

"Deal. Let's stop by the kitchen on the way out. I packed

you up a little treat to take home with you."

"I'm sure they won't survive the drive home, but I thank you. They were delicious as always."

Within a few minutes, he was in his car with a large container of cookies on the seat beside him. Waving as he backed out of the driveway, he felt a deep sense of satisfaction. He wasn't sure it was enough, but it was a start. He had loved his best friend like a brother, and he would do anything he could to honor him. Helping Kayleigh today had been such a small sacrifice for the man who had done so much for him. It made him smile as he thought about Robbie's face and how it would light up if he knew he had helped make Kayleigh's life a little easier. It had been a good day. He looked forward to spending another one just like it really soon.

Chapter Nineteen

April 2015

Trent was finally starting to feel like one of the guys. Even he knew how difficult it had been for the other firefighters to put up with him. He wanted to do something to make it up to them, but he was having trouble figuring out what exactly to do. He didn't want to risk doing the wrong thing, but letting fear rule him was a habit he had been trying to break for a long time, so he made a plan even though he could only hope it would work.

"What's so important you called us all into the kitchen?"

Hearing the slight impatience in Chief's voice almost made Trent lose his nerve, but he was determined to do something nice for all of them. Hoping he didn't look as nervous as he felt, he knew he had to move forward with his plan even though he couldn't ignore the slight trickle of sweat dripping down his back.

"Okay, I wanted everyone in here because I have something

I want to share with all of you." After Trent looked around to make sure he had their attention, he pushed the button on the projector he had set up for tonight. As everyone else turned their eyes to watch the scenes showing on the white wall, he dared to take a glance around to see what kind of reaction he was getting. He was worried at first because it seemed no one knew how to take his gesture. But, before long, he started to see smiles on almost every face as the men watched the slideshow he had prepared, each image reflecting the history of the station. When the pictures from the past few years ended the production, he actually heard several laughs followed by a sniffle or two. He knew why. One of the firefighters had died after a long battle with cancer a few years back. He had known seeing pictures with him in them would touch some of the veterans.

When the show ended, Trent turned off the projector as Chief turned the lights back on. He was pleased when he heard, "Well done, kid." This was followed by several pats on the back from most of the men. When Robert Wilson smiled at him from across the room and gave him a small salute, Trent knew he had finally been accepted as one of them.

And it was true. From that day on, he didn't seem to make as many mistakes and the guys suddenly found a spot for him at the kitchen table when they played a hand or two of poker. It felt good to belong even if he was the only one who knew it was just an act. Trent had never belonged anywhere. He didn't even feel like part of his own family, hadn't since he was a little boy. He had never managed to have a best friend and keeping a girlfriend had always been just out of his reach too. Without a dad who was able to teach him anything, he had never played on a sports team or learned to do the things boys need to know to grow up to be men. He had overheard enough of his teachers over the years to know he wasn't like other students either. Still, even if it wasn't real, it felt good to at least pretend to fit in at the fire station. He had long ago given up caring about any of that stuff anyway.

Chapter Twenty

May 1991

Mark couldn't get anything Robbie had told him out of his head. Why would his friend get involved with a girl so much younger than him? He didn't know any other guys who had girlfriends that young. If Robbie had kept her a secret, then obviously he even felt it was a bit creepy. He couldn't wrap his head around how much had happened in his friend's life in just a few months. Sarah's death seemed to be hitting him hard, and that made Mark believe that maybe there was more to his friend's secret than he had shared. He hated to do it, but he knew he needed to ask Robbie some tough questions. Not because he wanted to be nosy. No, it was more about helping him get out of this terrible funk he seemed to be sinking into a little deeper every day.

Picking up the phone from the small table beside his bed, Mark dialed the number he had memorized many years ago. When Robbie's mom picked up, he said the necessary pleasantries before asking to speak to his friend. It took a few minutes, but he finally heard a tired voice on the other end of the line say hello.

"Mark? What's up?"

"I just wanted to call and see if you want to go for a drive or something."

Waiting silently for an answer, Mark offered up a quick prayer. He would be lying if he said he wasn't worried, but he knew that was a fact he needed to keep to himself.

"Yeah, that would be good."

Keeping the relief out of his voice, Mark replied, "Pick you up in about 15 minutes then."

After they hung up, Mark bent over the side of the bed to put on the sneakers he had just kicked off a few minutes ago. Grabbing his wallet and car keys off the dresser, he headed out to confront his friend. He could only hope they would still be like brothers at the end of the drive. Even if it cost him everything, he knew asking the tough questions was the right thing to do. He only hoped he didn't end up regretting it after tonight.

After picking up milkshakes for their drive, Mark turned down the radio so they could talk without distractions, but Robbie beat him to it.

"Okay, I know you're dying to tell me something or ask me something, so just get it out."

Looking away from the road for just a second so he could see the look on his friend's face, Mark started, "Look, I know there's more to the story and I think you'll feel better if you get if off your chest. I can't make you tell me, but I think you should."

Waiting several seconds before opening his mouth again, Robbie rubbed his hand across his face before saying, "Yeah, there's more. A lot more. Sarah came by my house the day she got in the accident."

"I know that."

"Yeah, but there's more. I haven't been able to figure out Sarah's accident, but I know how she was feeling when she left my house That's the part I can't get out of my head. She found out about Meghan's abortion before I did, and to be honest, she was a lot more upset than I was about the whole thing. I honestly think I might be in shock about it all still, but I know I feel like a monster for dating someone so young. I feel like an idiot too. Sarah though, man, I just don't know how to explain her reaction to you. She lost it that day. She went on and on about how I ruined her life, how I used her just to get to Meghan, and finally how I killed her niece or nephew. By the time she got to the end of it all, she was crying so hard I had to go get a paper bag for her to breathe into. I've never seen anything like it. She really couldn't breathe. I'd be lying if I didn't say I was freaked out. Once she got under control, I could tell she was embarrassed by it all. She seemed to be really exhausted too. And then she gave me this one last look like she really hated me before she turned around and left. Through it all I barely said ten words, but she definitely knew I was mad at her too. I mean, she just would not stop yelling at me. I knew I deserved every word of it, and I tried my best to just take it. Somehow it made me feel like I was paying the price I deserved or something, but I still said some things that were really bad. I thought I was seeing her for the last time, but I didn't realize I was really seeing her for the last time. I still don't understand the accident though. Do you think she meant to die that way?"

Mark had been listening carefully as his friend unloaded for several minutes. It broke his heart to hear all of it. The fact that Robbie had probably caused all of this didn't stop what he felt. He could only feel sorry for him, for everyone involved in this big awful mess. He needed to be his best friend now, not his judge, so he answered, "Robbie, I don't know what to say right now. I don't think what you did was cool, but there's just no way to make it right. I wish I knew why Sarah died. I guess it's possible she did it on purpose, but I don't think so. Look, if she was that upset at your house, then it's possible she really wasn't over it when she left. I'm just guessing here, but you know the way you said she stopped breathing?"

Robbie couldn't help the tears he could feel slipping out of the corners of his eyes as he answered, "It was awful. She really scared me. I remembered seeing my grandma breathing into a bag one time, so I ran and got one for Sarah. I don't know how it works, but it seemed to help. And then she left so fast after she threw the bag down. I don't really know if she was okay or not when she drove off, but I know she was crying."

Mark continued, "So she probably really didn't have her breathing under control. If she had been driving when she had whatever kind of episode she had, would she have been okay?"

"I don't know, but I doubt it. So you think she started breathing, or not breathing, or whatever again? You think she did that again while she was driving? Man, I hadn't thought about that. But if it did happen like that then it really was an accident. But does that mean I caused it?"

"You didn't cause the accident, Robbie, but you were irresponsible getting involved with those girls. You can't turn back time though."

"I should go tell Sarah's parents what I did."

"Man, that's the last thing you need to do. You need to graduate, go to college, and forget Sarah and Meghan, okay?"

Robbie didn't answer. The only sound Mark heard was the

last drops of his friend's milkshake being sucked through the straw, then nothing but silence for the rest of their drive.

When Mark pulled into the driveway several minutes later, he turned and tried again, "Robbie, just put this behind you. I promise I won't ever tell anyone."

"But what about Meghan?"

"She's just a kid. It's an awful thing, but she's gonna grow up. When she does, she'll figure out that she's partly to blame for all of this too. One thing I'm pretty sure about is she won't tell anyone about any of it. By the time she's our age, you'll be graduating from college. This will blow over, and you really never have to see her again."

Not sure about the logic behind his friend's words, Robbie knew Mark was just trying to help. He also knew nothing would ever make him feel better again. But he did plan to take his advice. This had to be put behind him or he'd go crazy. He felt awful about Sarah's death, and he really wished he had never laid a hand on her sister, but there wasn't anything he could do about it now. Mark was right about one thing. He needed to put this all behind him, move to college, and forget any of it ever happened.

As Robbie got out of the car, he turned around to say one last thing, "I appreciate everything, you know? But I just can't keep talking about all of this."

When Mark reached over and fist bumped him, Robbie knew they had a pact. They never talked about Meghan or Sarah again. Until they had to. But that wouldn't happen for many years later when they both had grown into men and could clearly see how much they had both been boys when Sarah had died.

Chapter Twenty-One

May 2016

Five minutes after entering the kitchen, Kayleigh felt a wave of grief hit her so suddenly and with such ferocious strength that she had to physically bend over. When would it end? Having grown used to the dull pain she carried with her everywhere she went, these fresh stabs of grief overwhelmed her when they struck. She never seemed to be prepared for them.

Straightening back up, she forced herself to focus on the meal she no longer wanted to prepare. As she filled the red pasta pot with water, she averted her eyes from the sink, willing the memories to stay away. She was determined to not only fix this meal but to enjoy it. Becca would be coming over later, probably with a birthday cake to help her celebrate a day that used to be her favorite one all year. Now, instead of marking the passing of another year of life, it was just one more reminder of life without Robert. And lately all thoughts of her husband ended up at the same place, a place where she questioned everything she had ever thought was true about the man she had loved for nearly a quarter of a century. Things weren't adding up for her and she needed answers. She wasn't sure how much longer she could handle all of this. As if losing her husband wasn't bad enough, finding out he might have kept secrets from her was overwhelming.

*

Becca hesitated before knocking on the front door of her best friend's house. She knew Kayleigh would be at least a little depressed today, and she was fairly certain the cheesecake she was carrying in a box wrapped with a lavender silk bow wouldn't make her feel any better. But she had to at least try. After talking to her mom the other day, she figured Kayleigh needed more than just a sweet treat. She needed a friend who would encourage her to talk about all of this, really talk about it. And if her mom was right, Becca needed to dig a bit to help Kayleigh remember whatever it was she had forgotten. The trouble with her plan was that she was a terrible liar.

Opening the door, Kayleigh asked, "What's in the box?"

Becca smiled when she saw her friend's happy face, even though she didn't miss the barely noticeable hint of sadness hidden in her eyes, eyes that wouldn't quite meet her own. As she hugged her as they walked into the house together, she said, "Just something sweet for my sweetest friend on her birthday."

"Sounds perfectly delicious. Hand it over and grab two plates."

Becca went to the cabinet where the dessert plates were kept and grabbed two off the top of the stack. Reaching into the drawer for two forks, she said, "A huge slice for me please. Mimmo's makes the best cheesecake on the planet. I plan to enjoy every single calorie."

As they enjoyed the decadent treat together, Becca watched as her friend's face lost some of the heaviness she'd been carrying around lately. It hurt to see her looking this way. At first, right after Robert had died, Kayleigh had struggled just like Becca had known she would. But then she had gotten better, and it had seemed for a while that she was moving on a bit. Lately it was like she was no better off than she had been the day of the accident, and it was obvious to Becca that the dreams were the cause. She just had to find a way to get her to open up more, to talk about everything. She had to find a way to help her friend who was really more like a sister to heal. If only she could box up that healing in a white box and tie it with a pretty ribbon too. If only she could make everything better for her sweet friend.

Taking the plates and forks to the sink gave Becca the few seconds she needed to gather her courage before calling out, "Hey, Kayleigh? Want to sit out on the porch with some hot tea and just talk?"

When her friend entered the kitchen and silently started filling the kettle with water, she knew she had her answer. A few minutes later, when they were both settled in their lawn chairs and blowing on their cups of tea, Becca asked, "Do you remember when I told you about talking to my mom about your dreams?"

"Yes, I do. I've actually been thinking about that a lot lately."

"Do you think they're real? What I mean is, do you think she was right about memories surfacing?"

Kayleigh took a long sip of tea before turning in her chair to face Becca. "I do. At first, I thought Robert was really visiting me. I mean, deep down I knew he wasn't, but I thought somehow he was getting a message to me. I realize now that was just my grief talking, but I also think he had always wanted to share something with me, and now that's happening."

"Makes sense. I think Mom was right about hidden memories coming to the surface. I have no clue how you're really feeling, but do you think maybe part of your brain had to sort of shut off to deal with the grief? And maybe that allowed another part, the part where all these memories were hiding, to open up? Like that's where your dreams are coming from?"

"Becca, I've thought about these dreams more than I can tell you. What you're saying makes sense, but I'm just not sure it matters. It's like I'm hearing from Robert either way. I don't understand how I suppressed all these memories, but I'm grateful. I gotta tell you though, I have more questions now than answers. I can only hope for more dreams to help me figure out what he wanted me to know."

Becca set her empty cup on the table between them to free up her hands. Reaching out to hold her friend's shoulders, she asked, "But what if you never figure it out?"

"Then I'll be happy for what I've been given. I'll never understand why he was taken from me, but I know I have to focus on all we had. I just have to cling to that. I just have to."

"I agree. Now let's go inside. I'll help you clean up before I leave. You know you can always call me, right? If any of this gets to be too much, I'm here for you, even in the middle of the night."

Laughing as she got up to walk into the house with her best friend, Kayleigh said, "Now I know you really and truly love me. No one loves to sleep more than you, and if you're giving me permission to wake you up, that's huge."

Becca was glad to see a smile stay on Kayleigh's face for the rest of their visit. When she pulled out of the driveway about an hour later, she felt relief. Maybe her friend really was getting some closure. She could only hope that every memory her brain brought to the surface would be a good one. She wasn't sure if Kayleigh could handle it if anymore sadness came her way.

Chapter Twenty-Two

November 1991

Robert was getting used to living in the dorm with a bunch of guys. He was trying his best to keep his eyes off the girls, but he couldn't seem to get his new lab partner out of his mind. Kayleigh Beamon was almost like one of the guys, so much so that before he knew what was happening, they had become friends. When she asked him to go have pizza with her the first time, it had been easy to say yes. It never crossed his mind that anyone might think they were out on a date. It wasn't long before they were doing everything together. Robert was glad he had a good friend to help him get through freshman year. They shared more than just pizza those first few months of college. They told each other everything. Almost everything. Robert knew he had one secret that he would keep from everyone except the only two people who would ever know, at least if he had anything to do with it. Mark would never betray him, and Meghan had no reason to ever tell anyone either, but it still bothered him that he hadn't been there for her. He had taken Mark's advice about leaving it all behind him even if that meant finishing his senior year, graduating, and moving away to college without talking to her again. He told himself she would forget all about him. If only he could make himself believe his own lies and maybe even erase some of the guilt that seemed to follow him everywhere.

*

Kayleigh wished she could call her best friend about her feelings. She pictured them walking to the student union, grabbing a couple of coffees and maybe some of those chocolate muffins that were ridiculously good, and then finding a bench outside where they could visit. She would start talking and let go of everything that was begging release from her mind and heart. But, in her fantasy, her best friend was a girl who would understand boy troubles. A friend who would listen, ask the important questions like about how cute he was, and then get serious about finding an answer to Kayleigh's dilemma. But her biggest problem was the fact that her best friend was also the boy she was falling for.

She couldn't believe it had happened. When she and Robert had been paired up to work as lab partners together, she had definitely noticed his looks. It didn't take long for her to see past what was on the surface though. He was quiet, kind, and pretty much a goofball once you got him to open up. She was surprised at how comfortable he made her feel. When he didn't come on to her, she gradually forgot about his looks and got to know who he really was. The more time they spent together, the more she thought of him as her best friend. Until the day they were eating pizza together at a local place within walking distance of the campus, the day she finally admitted to herself what her heart had been trying to tell her all along. It sounded cliché even to her every time she played it back in her head, but she couldn't deny it if she tried. She had been starved that day, and that made her pretty much scarf down the first three slices. She didn't know she had left an embarrassing amount of grease on her chin until he reached over and gently swiped at it with the napkin he had just used to wipe his own mouth. Somehow the gesture was incredibly intimate, making it impossible to look at him for several seconds after it happened. Fortunately for her, Robert had been too busy eating his own pizza to notice. Once she had her heart under control, she took a risk and looked directly into his eyes. Seeing nothing new in his expression, she decided to keep her feelings to herself.

But, day after day, it got harder to be around him. She knew he had noticed how weird she was acting, and she had talked to him about it several times in her mind. She knew she would need to speak up soon before he started thinking she didn't like him anymore. That couldn't be further from the truth. The love she had felt for him as her best friend had somehow turned into true love, and it had happened without her even knowing it. So she found herself in the position of risking everything or gaining everything. What if he rejected her? Would they ever be able to stay friends? Even worse, what if she never told him how she felt only to learn later that he had been feeling it too? These thoughts kept her up more nights than she could count.

Chapter Twenty-Three

April 2015

Robert found himself wishing more and more that he had told Kayleigh everything back in college when they had only been friends. It would have hurt a lot less to lose her before he realized how much he loved her. Now, no matter how much he longed to tell her everything, he was just too scared. What if she walked away? What if, after all these years, when she found out he wasn't the person she had thought he was, she didn't have it in her to love him anymore? Knowing his wife like he did, he knew his mind was playing tricks on him. Kayleigh was the kindest, most compassionate woman he had ever met, but even nice people had their limits. So he lived with his deception every day, even while it ate away at him.

*

Kayleigh knew something was wrong with her husband, but she couldn't figure out what it was. He had always had these spells, had for as far back as she could remember. She didn't think he was even aware of what he was doing when they happened. He would get really quiet, staring at nothing at all for several seconds before jumping back into whatever he had been doing. It used to amuse her, but the longer they had been together the more the episodes had bothered her. There was something serious about the way he acted during these times, something that kept her from ever questioning him about it. She didn't know why she hadn't asked him about these times before, but she had her suspicions. There was a lot about her life as a foster child that she didn't want to talk about to anyone, a truth that had always made her sensitive to others. If she had to guess, she would say she had always assumed he would tell her when he was ready, and as the years passed, these strange episodes had just become part of who Robert was to her.

Watching him for a few seconds as he started shaving again, she turned to walk away. Maybe the best gift she could give him was the gift of silence, and if that meant she had to be invisible for a little while then she could participate in whatever this masquerade was. She loved him and knew he loved her. She trusted him with every fiber of her being, so she tiptoed out of the bathroom, leaving him alone with whatever thoughts had caused him to go so still. She hated that she couldn't help him with the sadness she always saw on his face when he did this, but she knew sometimes doing nothing was the kindest gesture of all.

*

Chief took a deep breath before he stood up from his desk. He knew Robbie had been struggling more than usual lately, and he had a feeling he knew why. It had been years since they had talked about what had happened when they were kids. He knew deep down that he wasn't responsible for anything that had happened back then, but that didn't keep him from thinking about it, and feeling guilty, from time to time. He wondered if he had said something different back then if maybe, just maybe, he could have saved his friend from the obvious pain he was in now. Even though Robbie thought he kept it hidden, it was there in his eyes when he thought no one was looking. The worse part for Chief was, even though he saw it, there was nothing he could say to help his friend. He had to do whatever he could to keep his fire station safe, and if that meant calling his best friend out, then that's what he would do, no matter how much he hated it. He had a job to do and a community to keep safe. And sometimes being the chief meant doing the uncomfortable task no one else would want to touch, so he did.

"Wilson."

When every man looked up, Chief only looked at one of them. He watched as Robbie sighed before standing up and walking toward him. Turning around, he went back to the chair behind his desk, listening for the sound of the door shutting behind his friend.

"Okay, Chief. You have my attention. That was a bit dramatic, don't you think?" Robert tried for a smile as he looked at the man he had known for most of his life. He stopped smiling when he focused on Chief's face and saw nothing but seriousness there.

"Robbie, you're not at your best lately. You sure you're up to working right now? I don't mind if you take some time off. Why don't you get Kayleigh to take some time off work too, maybe go away for a week or two? Might be good for you."

"I'm fine. Where is this coming from?"

"Look, we've been friends a long time, right? You don't ever say anything, but I can see it in your eyes when it comes back. And it's been eating at you for quite some time now."

"I'm not going to ask you what you're talking about. And I don't need time off. We done here?" Not waiting for an answer, Robert stood up and walked to the door, stopping before opening it but not turning back around.

Watching from his desk, Chief felt sorry for his friend. He knew not to push, but he had to finish saying what was on his mind. He had noticed more about Robbie than the way he was acting at work. He hadn't missed the way he had seemed a little distant the past few times they had gotten together to play poker or share a meal. Kayleigh seemed oblivious to it all, but he wondered if she sensed something was off too. The difference was, unlike his best friend's wife, he knew what was going on when Robbie got that faraway look in his eyes, so he spoke up, "Wait."

Stiffening, but still refusing to turn around, Robert's voice could barely be heard as he grumbled one word, "What?"

Standing up and walking toward him, Chief reached out and touched him on the shoulder before saying, "It's been a long time. Don't you think you need to let it all go? I hate seeing the guilt when it comes over you like this."

Finally turning around to face the man who knew all his secrets, Robert said, "How? How do I let this go? Do I call Meghan and invite her over to meet Kayleigh? How do I make this guilt go away without losing everything?"

Chief fought the tears that threatened to fall out of his eyes as he answered, "I don't know about Meghan. That seems a little dangerous to me. You know I've always thought it was a mistake to keep your past a secret from Kayleigh though. Look, you don't even know you do this, but sometimes you just go away for a bit."

"What in the world are you talking about? I don't go anywhere."

"No, not literally, but this look comes over you. The only way I know to describe it is you go back to the past. I can't believe Kayleigh's never questioned you about it."

"Well, she hasn't. How can I tell her about Meghan? You know we can't have children. Can you imagine how it will destroy Kayleigh if she finds out I actually had a baby? Well, not really, but you know what I mean. She will know for sure then that she's the reason we never had one. That will destroy her, and I love her too much to cause her that kind of pain. I don't want her to ever have any pain, much less any caused by me."

Chief looked toward his office door briefly before he continued by quietly adding, "Things have gotten more complicated now though."

Knowing exactly what his friend meant, Robert simply said, "Let me think about it some." Then he turned and walked out the door, letting it shut softly behind him.

Hoping he had at least planted a seed, Chief went back to his desk and paused to bow his head in prayer for a few seconds before going back to work. He knew it would take a miracle to help unload the heavy weight of guilt that had been on his friend's shoulders for over two decades. He also knew God could take it all away in an instant if Robbie would only ask. He prayed his friend would find the strength to do just that before it was too late.

*

Chief couldn't get his conversation with Robbie out of his head. Even now, after so much time had passed since they first talked about it, he knew his friend wasn't telling him the whole story. There was just something about the way he reacted that always confirmed his suspicions. Robbie seemed to want to share more, but he always held back. Chief had tried his best to keep the promise he made so long ago, but the agony that fell across his friend's face was telling. If only he would open up, then maybe just talking about it could bring him the relief he obviously needed. But Chief knew better than to pry any more than he already had. He had known his friend long enough to understand what his past had cost him, but lately he found himself worried his past might end up costing him his future with Kayleigh. It broke Chief's heart to have his hands tied about the whole thing.

Chapter Twenty-Four

June 2016

Kayleigh was grateful she had been free of the dreams for several nights in a row. Getting a good night's sleep was a welcome change, but making her way through each day was proving to be a challenge. Being so well-rested in the morning gave her a boost of energy she hadn't felt since Robert had died. It also gave her more time to think. She was learning that having too much time to think wasn't always a good thing.

Becca's words of wisdom seemed to be true because memories she had obviously buried long ago were popping up left and right. Snippets of a conversation she had forgotten, a subtle look that had once crept across her husband's face, and even a shocking memory of hearing Robert blurt out a name while sleeping, it all just kept entering her mind. Almost more surprising than these memories was the realization that she had forgotten them in the first place. She could only believe the shock of losing her husband had somehow jarred them loose.

The dreams had been a catalyst for bringing them to the surface of her mind, and she was struggling with knowing how to deal with it all. Sometimes she wished they had just stayed buried.

Texting Becca for the fourth time in less than an hour, Kayleigh decided she couldn't wait any longer to talk to someone. Scrolling through her contact list, she paused when she saw Becca's mom's name. Although she had a good relationship with the older woman, she wasn't sure if it was the best idea to reach out to her now. Unable to resist, she sent a quick message asking Mrs. Jones to please meet her for coffee later in the day. When Becca's mom immediately texted back a time and a place, Kayleigh breathed a sigh of relief. She needed someone to talk to. In fact, as she sent yet another text to her best friend, she hoped all three of them would soon be joining hands for a quick prayer before having a much-needed chat. She hoped they could help her figure everything out.

*

When she finally looked at her phone, Becca was surprised to see how many missed messages were on the screen. She had left it in her purse while she was sitting in the chair at her dentist's office. Not wanting anything to interrupt this appointment she had put off for far too long, she had made sure to turn her phone to silent. After paying for the visit and returning to her car, the first thing she did was to look at its screen. Seeing several messages from her best friend and one from her mom didn't alarm her. Kayleigh was acting more like herself lately, and if she had sent a string of texts in a short amount of time, it was probably all good news. Smiling at the thought of seeing the silly memes her friend used to be known for, Becca was surprised to see increasingly frantic texts about some kind of memories Kayleigh seemed desperate to discuss. Reading through them all quickly, she turned her attention to the one her mom had sent. Reading about the coffee date, Becca glanced at the time. If she drove straight there, she would only be a few minutes late. As much as her numb mouth didn't want to think about sipping a cup of coffee, she was more than willing to sit at a table across from the two most important women in her life if it meant helping Kayleigh heal.

Pulling up to the coffee shop several minutes later, Becca smiled when she looked through the window and saw her mom reach over to gently pat Kayleigh's hand. It was easy to see the worry on her dear friend's face. She found herself once again wishing she could turn back time and bring Robert back to his wife. She still couldn't wrap her head around how a veteran firefighter had died by falling out a window. She knew the investigation had been thorough, so she had no choice but to accept the results. Still, none of it made sense to her. Robert had been a strong man in the prime of his life. He had also been one of the smartest people she had ever met. The notion of him running into a window with enough force to break the glass had never added up to her, but she would never dream of bringing up such a painful topic to her grieving friend. No matter how much time passed, she kept coming back to that night in her mind. Something wasn't right, but she had accepted the fact that even if they found out it wasn't an accident, nothing would bring Robert Wilson back.

Chapter Twenty-Five

May 1991

Sarah wanted to kick herself. She had wasted so much time worrying about Robbie, actually wanting to help him with his pain over the breakup he caused. She knew her sister was hurt too, but she had no idea how much. Finding out about the baby had devastated her. Her sister was much too young to have dealt with any of this, especially without support. She wished Meghan had asked her for help. She would have told her to stay away from the guy if she had only known what he was capable of, and even if she hadn't been able to convince her little sister to not sleep with the older boy, at least she could have been there for her when the pregnancy test showed a pink line. And the thought of her little sister going into a clinic alone to have an abortion hurt the most of all. She knew Meghan, knew what an innocent girl she really was. There was no way she would have followed through with the procedure if she had understood what it really meant. Listening to her sister cry night after night told her that Meghan had finally figured out what she had done. It made her sick to think it all could have been easily prevented. And the fact that they no longer shared secrets hurt more than she ever could have imagined.

The one time Meghan had opened up to her, Sarah had been surprised by how much she had matured. But she knew it shouldn't be a surprise at all. Considering all the things her sister had been doing lately, it explained how little she resembled the girl who had teased her about having a crush on an older boy just a few short months ago.

*

"Meghan, just talk to me."

Looking at her big sister made her want to cry. She felt like such a disappointment. At first, she had tried to ignore feeling like a traitor, but then she got caught up in being Robbie's girlfriend. It hadn't even bothered her that he had asked her to keep it all a secret. It made her feel like Juliet to his Romeo. Things got out of hand quickly though, and then he dumped her like she hadn't meant anything at all. She had been so scared, but she hadn't known who to turn to. And now a day didn't go by that she didn't wonder if she had made a mistake. She couldn't handle thinking about it all, so she ignored everyone, even her best friend who just happened to be her sister. But now, looking into those eyes that were so much like her own, she wanted to talk. Maybe letting it out a little at a time wouldn't be too bad. She knew better than to tell her everything; Sarah couldn't handle hearing it all, at least not yet.

"Sarah, it's like meeting Robbie was like getting a gift that wasn't mine to open. The wrapping was just so pretty and shiny, and I honestly only wanted to peek inside at first. Then I got carried away when he started paying attention to me. I was awful, wasn't I?" Pausing to look at her sister again, she only saw love, the kind she needed to see to keep talking, so she did, "Things got out of control fast. It was like on Christmas morning when we used to rip open all our gifts as fast as we could. Do you remember that? Of course, you do. Man, it was only a few years ago. Anyway, remember how sometimes we couldn't even find some of the gifts because we had lost them in our excitement to open the ones that grabbed our attention the most? There was just a ridiculous amount of gift wrap everywhere."

Not wanting to stop her sister from sharing, yet knowing she needed to encourage her, Sarah simply said, "Yeah, I remember."

"Well, I lost me when I ripped open the gorgeous gift that was Robbie Wilson. I really did. I lost sight of everything. And you know what the most awful part is? What was inside was ugly. It was such a letdown. I didn't enjoy being with him, felt so dirty every time. And the way he dumped me was the worst of it. I didn't even have a chance to tell him about, you know. It's not like he just rejected me, Sarah. He did so much more. He made me feel invisible. He dumped me like I was nothing. It was like he was putting the trash out or something. I felt completely alone when I left his house that day. I always thought someone hating me would be the most pain I would ever feel, but I was so wrong. Someone not noticing you, not caring about you enough to even hate you, hurts so much worse."

Once she knew Meghan had said all she wanted to say, Sarah reached out to pull her into a hug as she told her, "Oh Meg, he's such a jerk. Now listen, I'm not trying to say he isn't the terrible person we both know he is, but I have to tell you something. He's miserable. I see him at school, and he definitely is thinking about you." Feeling the way her sister moved a little as they hugged, she was quick to add, "But I don't want you to contact him. Let him get over you. He's not worth your time."

Meghan pulled out of the hug, using her sleeve to wipe the wetness off her face, before whispering, "I could never be with him again. I don't want to ever talk to him again, but am I wrong? Should I tell him about, you know?" The sobs that stole her breath were pitiful.

Sarah wished more than anything she could take the pain for her sister, but she knew this was one thing Meghan would have to truly deal with on her own. But, as she reached out to hug her again, she knew she would always be around to listen, no matter how many times her sister needed to tell her story. She had one more thing to say, "Meghan, don't tell him. No good can come from it, okay?"

Hearing their mom calling them to dinner, both girls went into the bathroom together to wash their faces. They didn't need to talk about keeping this all a secret from their parents. Some things sisters just knew, and this was definitely one of them. Looking at Meghan in the mirror, Sarah felt a rage building inside of her like she had never known. Yes, she would be the listener and keeper of secrets that her sister needed her to be, but she was going to do one other thing too. She was going to pay that jerk a visit, one he would never forget.

Chapter Twenty-Six

June 2016

Becca knew if she just stayed quiet, her mom would get Kayleigh to open up. And she knew her best friend needed to share what was on her heart with someone. She tried not to feel jealous, but she couldn't deny the gift with people her mom had. She smiled as she remembered how perfect strangers used to talk her mother's ears off whenever they were in line behind them at the grocery store. What would have been a casual conversation between two strangers if one of them wasn't her mother often turned into several minutes of therapy. The other person always felt compelled to thank her mother with a hug, often while tears streamed down both of their faces. Becca remembered being in awe of her mom's ability to simply listen before sharing a few words of encouragement that always seemed to hit home. Yes, she still fought jealousy from time to time, but the older she got the more she simply loved her mom for being who she was. And she felt incredibly blessed to be her daughter.

"Okay, so I can see how these dreams are a bit disturbing, but there's more, isn't there?"

Kayleigh let her eyes drift toward her best friend and gave her a small smile. She wondered if Becca knew how wonderful her mom was. Somehow, looking at the pride on her best friend's face, she knew she did. Looking back at the older woman, she answered, "Yes, there's more. I think I always knew Robert was keeping something from me. He would look away sometimes and, I don't know, go somewhere without me. We never once talked about it. I see now how that was a big mistake on my part, but I think I was scared about what he would share. Somehow, over the years, I must have picked up bits and pieces though. And now I think my brain is using these dreams to help me put it all together, but you know what? It's really exhausting, and I just don't know if I have the strength to follow this through to the end."

"Here's what I think. It's too much because, well, it's too much. Like literally. You're dealing with a couple of decades of bits and pieces. I suggest you take them one at a time. Deal with one piece before you move onto the next. It will be like one of those puzzles you love to put together. You don't dump a thousand pieces out expecting to see the whole picture. Same is true here. Put this puzzle together one piece at a time and eventually you will see the big picture."

Kayleigh looked at Becca again and said, "You know your mom's a genius, right?"

Becca reached out to give her mom's hand a squeeze as she smiled and said, "She's the best."

"You two are the sweet ones. Now, let's get a refill of this delicious coffee and talk about this new man my daughter's dating. Wait right here. I'll be back with the coffee in a minute."

Laughing out loud at the look on her friend's face, Kayleigh said, "A new boyfriend? When did this happen?"

"It hasn't. At least not yet. I met this guy, and he asked me out. Our first date is this weekend. How do you think my mom even knows about it already?"

"Like I said, the woman's a genius."

Later, after they had discussed this mystery man, they all left the coffee shop together, promising to get together again soon. Kayleigh liked the way that made her feel. She also was looking forward to going home to work on the puzzle of her dreams. Maybe if she wrote about each piece she would finally see the whole picture. As much as she still loved her husband, she was ready to put all of this behind her. It was time to move forward a bit more and whatever this secret was could only hold her back. Her husband's past wasn't somewhere she wanted to hang around for long; she knew Robert wouldn't want her to linger there either.

*

Kayleigh woke up screaming. After writing about her dreams for a couple of hours last night, she had taken a relaxing bubble bath before bed. She had only been kidding herself when she closed her eyes and softly said, "Tonight there will be no dreams." If she had only known that a dream could feel so much like a living nightmare, she would have done anything to stay awake. This one was different from the rest. Robert wasn't in it, but she had thought about him the entire time. She had been in a car, driving much too fast, and when she hit something, it woke her up. Her heart was beating so hard, and she wasn't even completely sure who she was when she opened her eyes and looked frantically around her bedroom.

The more she thought about it, the more she realized whoever she was in the dream had been in a car accident. The entire time she had been driving all she could think about was Robert, but she called him Robbie in the dream. And she was furious at him, much more so than she ever had been in real life. This was worse even than her earlier dream when she woke up wanting to punch him. This time she knew she had a real reason to hate him, but the dream ended before she found out what he had done to make her feel such hatred toward him.

She was sure she had just been given another piece of the puzzle and she was determined to figure out where it fit. There was something in her husband's past just begging to be discovered. She hoped she could figure it out before long because she wasn't sure how many more dreams like the one she had last night she could bear. Waking up scared wasn't her idea of a good time, and she was sure it wasn't what Robert would want for her if he were still alive.

*

"Becca, can you swing by sometime this week? I've written down everything I can remember from each of my dreams, and I seriously need a pair of fresh eyes. I can't help but feel like I'm getting close to the truth."

"How about later tonight? I have dinner plans, but I'll be free after."

Giggling just a little, Kayleigh answered, "Dinner plans, huh? I want to hear all about those dinner plans before we discuss my dreams. Have fun."

"You're worse than my mom. It's not like that. Kevin and I are just friends. I hoped for more, but it's just not like that."

"Sure. Whatever you say. See you later tonight."

"I'll text when I'm on my way."

Deciding to heat up some leftovers before looking at her so-called puzzle again, Kayleigh headed into the kitchen to see what she could find in the refrigerator. Settling on a slice of pizza and a serving of lasagna, she was soon curled up on the couch enjoying her meal. As she munched on the cheese and green pepper pizza that had always been her favorite, she found herself wishing for another piece. It felt good to have her appetite back. She was ready for everything in her life to get back to normal. She could only hope Becca would be able to make more sense out of her most recent dream than she had been able to.

A couple more hours passed before she heard a car pull up in her driveway. The chocolate chip cookies she had made were cooling on the counter just waiting for her and Becca to enjoy a few. Opening the front door, she grinned when she saw how dressed up her friend was. As she hugged her, she caught a definite whiff of perfume. Just friends, huh? She didn't believe Becca now any more than she had earlier when they had talked on the phone, but she would give her friend a break. There would be plenty of time later to tease her. She had a puzzle to solve now and no time to add her friend's love life to her problems.

"I smell cookies. Girl, you're going to make me gain ten pounds, you know that?"

"Even though I bake them, I'm smart enough to know how good they are. Let's go eat a ridiculous amount and then I want you to tell me what these dreams mean."

"Deal."

After they had both enjoyed an uncomfortable amount of her signature dessert, they made their way to the den where Kayleigh had set up her new puzzle table. Instead of a thousand tiny puzzle pieces, there were several pages of notes, each written in a different color ink.

Becca sat down and started reading the page written in blue. "Does it matter what order I read these?"

Shaking her head as she sat down at the table with her friend, Kayleigh answered, "Not really. I haven't been able to figure out a timeline of my memories. If you look in the upper right corner of each page though, you'll see a number. I did keep the dreams in chronological order. It seems like there must be a reason for the order of the dreams, but I sure haven't been able to figure that out yet."

After reading for about twenty minutes, Becca felt like she had an idea. She just wasn't sure if she should share it out loud yet. Even though Robert had been gone over a year now, she knew her friend well enough to know the pain was still very much fresh. She chose her next words carefully as she said, "I think there might be a reason for the order. I could be wrong, but do you want to hear the theory I've come up with?"

Sighing, Kayleigh admitted, "I'm not sure I want to hear anything. Don't take this the wrong way, but I'm not sure I want to know whatever this all is. I'd be lying if I said I'm ready to know what Robert's big secret was. Part of me wants the dreams to stop, but another part is scared. Becca, if I stop dreaming about Robert, will I one day forget about him? Will I forget how he looked, the sound of his voice, the way his arms felt around me? I just don't know if I could stand it if any of that happened."

"Oh Kayleigh, I don't know what's gonna happen. It seems like closure will be a good thing though, right?"

"I guess so. Go ahead. I promise not to interrupt you. Please tell me whatever you've come up with. I really want to hear what you're thinking. Actually I'm not sure what I want. Oh, I'm sorry. Please tell me what you've figured out."

"Okay. Here goes. It's just the impression I'm getting from these notes though. I don't know anything other than what you've told me. I wish I did, but I don't. First, let's look at the order of these dreams. Your first one was where you learned how a mother loves a child, then you saw Robert as a little boy, so those first two dreams were great, right?"

"They were wonderful. I'm not exaggerating when I say they were a balm to my soul. I loved Robert so much when he was alive. I still do, but after those two dreams, there was a different level of love in my heart. It was a gift I needed more than I knew."

"And that's all great, really it is, but then the dreams shifted, right? I think those first couple of dreams were God's way of making sure you remembered how much you loved Robert. But then the rest of the dreams were where the truth started to be revealed. You doing okay?"

"I'm good. Keep going."

"Well, you started dreaming about parts of Robert's life you didn't know about. You already knew he loved his momma, and you knew he had a childhood too, but learning about girls from high school and the mysterious woman in the coffee shop had to be uncomfortable. I definitely think he kept a whopper of a secret from you, but I also think he wanted to tell you. I suspect he let little tidbits slip out once in a while, probably because he really wanted you to know. That's it. That's all I've got."

"So, do you think I really saw him in our coffee shop? Like maybe I blocked it from my memory?"

"I don't know. I wish I did."

"Thanks Becca. I wish I knew the whole story. I really wish there was someone I could ask. If only Robert's parents hadn't died. I imagine they would know something."

"Is there anyone else? Anyone who might know?"

Kayleigh's eyes widened as she looked at her friend before saying, "I can't believe I'm just now thinking about this. Chief and Robert were friends from way back. They met when they were like five or six years old. If anyone would know, it would be him."

"There you go. I think you should go talk to him. But Kayleigh? Don't go talk to him until you're ready to hear the truth. Chief might just tell you more than you want to know."

"I'll sleep on it."

"I would tell you to have sweet dreams, but I don't think that would make you feel any better."

"Speaking of sweet and dreamy, it's time for you to fess up. Your mom's not here, so spill. Why are you and this mystery man just friends? Don't hold back. I want to hear everything."

Chapter Twenty-Seven

May 1991

Sarah woke up in a bad mood. Listening to Meghan cry again last night had been too much. Deciding to go see Robbie after work tonight made her feel a little bit better. If nothing else, it would give her satisfaction to see fear in his eyes. He needed to know how much suffering he had caused, and she was just the person to tell him. Sure, it meant getting home past her curfew, but she could handle whatever punishment her parents decided to dish out. She just couldn't handle one more day of holding in the words she needed to say to him. She was tired of pretending not to know the pain her sister felt in her heart. She was tired of the tears she saved for when she was alone.

It took forever for school to end, and then her shift at work passed just as slowly, but soon she was in her car headed to see Robbie. She hadn't bothered to let her folks know she would be late, and she certainly had no intention of letting Meghan know what she was going to do. She had to say what was on her heart, what had been eating away at her. Once she found some relief, then she would do everything in her power to help her sister find some too. She still couldn't believe Meghan had gotten pregnant, and she couldn't let herself think about the rest. She had never discussed the details with her, but Sarah had known enough girls at school who had been pregnant one day but not the next. Imagining her baby sister doing the same thing almost was too much to bear.

Pulling onto Robbie's street several minutes later almost made her lose her nerve. Seeing his truck in the driveway made her mad. He had taken her out on dates in that truck, leading her to believe they had something special. The way he dumped her like she was nothing still stung, but nothing topped what he did to her sister. Stopping her car just short of his bumper made a small smile cross Sarah's face. He loved that truck, but she didn't care all that much about the hand-me-down car her parents had given her for her sixteenth birthday. It took all her self-control not to inch forward just another foot or so. She knew scratching his truck was an immature thing to do, and she just didn't want to stoop to his level, so she resisted.

A few minutes later she was ringing the doorbell, making pleasant small talk with Mrs. Wilson while waiting to confront the person she hated more than anyone else in the world. Seeing the confused look on Robbie's face when she walked into his room a few minutes later didn't give her the sense of satisfaction she had thought it would.

"Sarah? Why are you here?" Robbie couldn't help the gruffness he heard in his own voice.

"Meghan. How could you? Do you have any idea what you've done?"

Grabbing her arm, he pulled her into his room, not wanting his mom to hear the way Sarah's voice was all high-pitched and shaky. It was obvious that she was upset, but it was more than that. She was nervous in a way he had never seen her before. He knew he needed to just let her say what was on her mind, get her out of his house, and be done with her. If only he had dated girls his own age like his other friends did. He had been such an idiot and now he was paying for it.

"Let go of me. I mean it. Don't you dare touch me."

"Sarah, you're upset. I need you to calm down and tell me why you're here."

"You're joking, right? You use me and then dump me for my kid sister. That alone is enough reason for me to be upset. But what you did to Meghan? You should be arrested for that, but she won't tell our parents. You ruined her life. You get that, right?"

Slamming his hand down on his dresser hard enough to bounce his phone to the floor, Robbie barely controlled his voice as he told her, "You're being a bit dramatic, don't you think? All I did was dump her. How in the world would that ruin her life? You're crazy, you know that, right?"

"Dramatic? You aren't the one listening to my sister cry herself to sleep every night. You aren't the one who has to keep this all a secret from our parents. You aren't..."

When Sarah bent over gasping for breath, Robbie changed his tone, "Hey, are you okay? Look, do you need to sit down or something?" When she didn't seem able to respond, he remembered something he had seen his grandmother do.

Running downstairs to the kitchen as fast as he could without getting his mom involved, he opened the drawer where she kept things like sandwich bags and tin foil. Finding what he was looking for, he got back to his room as fast as he could and told her, "Sarah, breathe into this." Holding the paper bag over her mouth and nose, he watched as she slowly got herself under control.

Within a few minutes, she pushed the bag away from her face and hit Robbie's arm to get him away from her. Tears pouring from her eyes, she choked out, "Meghan isn't old enough to drive a car, but she had an abortion because of you. You've ruined her life!" Running out of his room before he had a chance to answer her, she was out of the house and in her car in less than a minute. Cranking the car, she peeled out of his driveway without even bothering to see if there were any other cars on the road. She knew she was being reckless, but she just didn't care.

As she drove, she played her conversation with Robbie over and over in her head. She didn't notice when she was twenty miles over the speed limit, but she did notice when she started having trouble breathing again. It scared her, and she didn't know how to get the relief she had gotten when she had breathed into that paper bag. Grabbing her chest, she closed her eyes as her panic made her lose control of the wheel. By the time she realized she had drifted into the other lane, she could see the bright headlights of the truck headed straight for her. But it was too late. The last thought to go through her mind when her car slammed into the much larger vehicle was of Meghan. She had let her sister down again.

Chapter Twenty-Eight

July 2016

Trent took one last look at his bunker gear before walking out of the fire station. He never should have taken this job. He had honestly thought he could make it work. He had obviously never been more wrong about anything in his life. He could tell Chief didn't completely understand why he was quitting, just like he also knew the older man was holding back. It had been apparent that he wanted to say more, but he had restrained himself. For that, Trent was grateful.

*

Chief watched the younger man as he walked out of the station. He wondered what he could have done differently. He knew Robbie had done his best to mentor the kid even though, at first, he hadn't exactly been keen about the idea. He had to let Trent go though. Whatever good Robbie had started was just going to have to be enough. Chief wished he could tell the rookie everything he knew, but he was afraid it would only cause him more pain. As usual, where his friendship with Robbie was concerned, he had to keep it all a secret, so he let the kid keep walking.

*

Kayleigh smiled at the young firefighter as they passed in the parking lot of the station. She was sure he knew who she was, so she was surprised when he didn't acknowledge her. Then she remembered how it had been with Robert. Some days he had gotten home late, and when she asked about it, he told her he had needed to drive around a bit just to clear his head. Always determined to leave work at the station, he told her some shifts stuck with him more than others. She offered up a quick prayer for Trent Jefferson. She suspected he was feeling what Robert had felt so many nights after work. No wonder he hadn't felt like talking to her.

Walking into the station made her smile. She could feel her husband in this place. He had been so happy here. She would never stop being sad that he had died, but somehow it made it a little less painful to know he had died doing something he truly loved.

Knocking on Chief's office door a few seconds later made the smile slip from her face. She wasn't looking forward to this conversation. If she were being honest with herself, she was a little afraid of what he would tell her. Part of her hoped he wouldn't have any insight into her dreams, but a bigger part, the one had made her come see him today, hoped he would. She needed to know whatever it was about her husband's past that he had been desperate to tell her. She wished more than anything that she had been a bit more sensitive to his needs. She could clearly remember now the times he had seemed to want to talk to her, but there was no turning back time. No, all she could do was try to find out what she could from the only person who knew her husband as well as she did, maybe better in some ways.

"Kayleigh, I wasn't expecting you. Is everything okay?"

Grateful for the genuine concern on the man's face, she reached out to give him a hug before asking, "I hope this is a good time?"

"Of course. I was just working on some personnel paperwork, but it can wait. No one tells you how much time you'll spend at a desk when you get promoted to chief, you know?"

"I guess I've never really thought about that."

"Never mind me. I know you didn't pop in to discuss my job. Can I get you something to drink?"

"Maybe some water?"

When Chief left the office to grab them both a bottle of water from the kitchen, Kayleigh realized what she really needed was a few moments to compose herself more than she needed the drink. This wasn't going to be easy for either of them if Chief actually did know some of her husband's secrets, but she just had to ask him, no matter how much pain it caused them both.

"Here you go." Handing her a bottle before he opened his own, Chief took a long swallow before settling into his seat and asking, "What can I help you with?"

Attempting a smile, Kayleigh sat forward in the chair before telling him about the dreams. She was grateful he didn't interrupt her, grateful he maintained eye contact with her. She never saw a smile cross his face, but she knew he was intelligent and would process everything she told him before passing judgement. She ended with, "Chief, you knew Robert longer than I did. You knew him when he was that little boy in my dream just like you knew him when he was a teenager. Does anything I'm describing to you make sense?"

Rarely at a loss for words, he didn't know what to say to her. Looking at the hopeful way her eyes lit up was what did it. He just couldn't deny her the measure of peace she seemed so desperate for. He knew he couldn't answer all of her questions, but he was determined to at least set her on the right path.

Clearing his throat, he simply asked, "Are you sure you want to know?"

With that one question, Kayleigh felt her heart stop beating for a second. So there was a secret. There really was something her husband had kept from her. And his best friend had known about it all along. She felt betrayed and hurt at the same time, certain the emotions were playing out on her face, but she wanted to know. Needing to give him an answer, she simply whispered, "Yes, I do."

"You need to know that Robbie was determined to leave his past behind him when we moved away to college. He had led a pretty normal life until his senior year. Don't get me wrong. The guy was crazy popular. He was the basketball star and all that. Girls were always trying to pick him up. I'm so sorry to have to tell you that, but it's the truth. He kept his wits until our last year of high school though. He met this girl. She was a bit younger and they only dated for a little while before he dumped her."

Kayleigh interrupted to ask, "Was her name Sarah?"

Seeing the shocked recognition on his face was all the answer she needed. Instead of answering her, he quickly asked, "How did you know?"

"I'm honestly not sure. That was the name of the girl in my dream, but I know I must have heard her name sometime throughout our marriage. Maybe Robert called it out in his sleep. Maybe his mom talked about her. I have no memory of ever hearing her name until the dream though."

"Wow, that's wild. When I was listening to you talking about your dreams a minute ago, I guess it didn't click how real they were. Man. That must have been rough for you to deal with. Especially since you're also dealing with losing Robbie. I'm just so sorry about all this."

"It's not your fault, and you're actually helping me now so much more than you'll ever know. Please keep telling me what you can. Anything will help me. Truly."

"Well, Kayleigh, it gets worse. I want you to be prepared, okay?" When she nodded, he went on, "He dumped this girl Sarah for her younger sister, but I didn't know it at the time. I guess Robbie kept it a secret because most high school seniors don't date eighth graders. Maybe he was ashamed, but I can't tell you that for sure. I know they dated for a few months before he dumped her too."

"I can't believe it. He sounds so cruel."

"Kayleigh, it wasn't like that. High school guys are jerks, you know? And he seriously had a big head. He had been built up for almost four years. Getting put on the varsity team as a freshman ended up being too much of a boost for his ego, but trust me, he paid for it. The rest is a bit fuzzy, but I'll tell you what I know. Sarah and Meghan, that's the other girl, were crazy close. One night Sarah went to Robbie's house to confront him. She lost it according to him. Well, that night, she got into a car accident."

"An accident?" When all the color left her face, Chief jumped up from his chair and went to her. Instructing her to lower her head between her knees, he gently reached his fingers around her wrist to check her pulse. Once he was sure she was okay, he went back to his seat.

"Kayleigh, maybe we should stop for now."

"Tell me this. Was it a head-on collision?"

"How on earth did you know that? Wait, your dream? That's too weird. But yeah, it was. It was declared an accident, but Robbie wasn't too sure. I personally think it was because she had some kind of panic attack at his house before she raced off in her car. Common sense always told me she had lost control of the car because she was having trouble breathing. Robbie never stopped blaming himself though. Sometimes I'd catch him staring at nothing at all, and I knew where he was. In his mind he went back to that awful time. We never talked about it much. Maybe twice in twenty years or something. It just wasn't a place he could visit again, you know?"

"Is that all?"

Knowing it wasn't, but also recognizing his friend's widow had suffered enough, he decided to spare her any more pain, even if it meant lying to her. "Yeah, that's all."

When Kayleigh stood up to leave, he couldn't help but notice the way she looked defeated. He hoped he had done the right thing. Asking her if she would be okay, he had to be satisfied with the quick hug she gave him before she left his office. Glancing up at the ceiling, he wondered if his friend would be glad to finally have this out in the open. He was afraid of the answer. For the first time since the accident, he was glad Robbie wasn't alive. He wasn't sure his friend could handle seeing the pain on his wife's face as she left the station. He felt so bad knowing he had been the one to put it there.

Chapter Twenty-Nine

June 1991

Robbie couldn't focus on what was happening around him. Sure, he had been to a funeral before, but it was always an old person in the casket. It was more than the fact that this funeral was for someone close to his own age. He had known her. He had been the last person to see her alive. The guilt was too much. He had only looked at the front row once, barely able to see the heads of her parents over the crowd of people packed into the funeral home. He was grateful he didn't have to see Meghan again even though he knew she was up there with the rest of Sarah's family.

Trying not to react when his mom pinched his leg, Robbie got the message. She knew he was fidgeting, but she would never guess why. He needed this to end so he could move on with his life. He was grateful graduation was right around the corner. Leaving for college couldn't happen soon enough.

When it came time to offer condolences to the family, he

bent down to tell his mom he needed to be excused. Trying to ignore her frown, he walked back to where he knew the bathrooms were, but instead of going into one, he kept walking until he felt fresh air hit his face. His parents would just have to figure out he was waiting for them at the car. He needed time to think and more space than the stuffy building offered.

His mom hadn't been in the car for more than two seconds before she asked, "Robbie, are you okay?"

Pleased to hear more concern than irritation in her voice, he knew he could spin this to his advantage. "Mom, I'm sorry. I just couldn't deal with any of that right now."

From his vantage point in the back seat of their sedan, he didn't miss the look that passed between his parents. He wasn't surprised when his dad joined the conversation and said, "Son, if there's anything you want to talk about, anything at all, your mother and I are here. Just let us know, okay?"

"Dad, it's all good. It was just weird going to the funeral of someone I actually know. I don't need to talk, but thanks. Really. I appreciate you two."

They rode in silence the rest of the way home. When Robbie jumped out of the car and ran into the house, no one tried to stop him. He was glad his room was down the hall from the one his parents shared. He had no idea how he would explain the way he cried himself to sleep. He just knew he had to move to college soon. He never wanted to think about Sarah and Meghan again.

Chapter Thirty

August 2016

Becca saw the journal on the puzzle table and glanced across the room. Kayleigh was looking at the notes she had been working on for months and didn't notice the way her friend was staring at her.

"Hey, you've been writing again?"

Kayleigh looked up when she heard the softness in Becca's voice. She breathed deeply before offering a response, "I have. I kind of got back into it when I started making notes about all my dreams. And then one night I started pouring out all my feelings into this journal. I'm not quite writing poetry again like I used to, but this is some pretty deep stuff."

"Anything you want to share?"

Kayleigh's laugh didn't exactly sound happy when she answered, "Sure, but be careful what you ask for. You may not like what you read."

Giving her friend a hug as she grabbed the journal off the puzzle table and took it with her to the couch, Becca braced herself for what she was about to read. Nothing could have prepared her for the pain on the pages.

A piece of my heart has been ripped from my chest making it impossible for me to be who I once was. I'm no longer whole. Yet I live in a world surrounded by people who expect me to be. People who don't understand the constant ache, the constant emptiness that weighs me down. How can having part of me gone make me heavier instead of lighter? But it's true. Sometimes I almost fall under the weight of it all. I stumble, but I stay upright. I have a smile on my face that fools everyone because no one looks closely enough to see that it never quite reaches my eyes. Only I know that looking the same on the outside is an unfair reflection of who I've become without you. I don't recognize myself anymore, but that's something I can't share with anyone. No one wants to see.

I miss you. It hits me out of nowhere with a force I can't explain. I long to hold you, to touch you, to see you close up so I can convince myself that you're real. I don't dare slip back where my memories long to take me. *The pain is still too real, too fresh, too raw. It's a wound that rips open every day, refusing to heal. And I don't want it to. I can't hold you to feel you, so I settle for the pain, understanding my needs are invisible to everyone who isn't me. If you were here, I know you would see straight through it all and focus on my pain. And with one smile you would take it away.*

But even if I could see you right now, I know it wouldn't be the same. We've both changed. If I could see you like I desperately wish for, we would have to ease back into what we had, both of us aware of the subtle differences between who we were and who we now are.

I can't see you. At least not now. So I cling to the hope of the tomorrow that I long for, even though I know it won't actually be the tomorrow that will follow tonight's fitful sleep. And probably not the next one or the next. I can't turn to a page in my calendar and find where I've penciled it in. No, my calendar is full of seemingly empty pages. Full of empty days. Days heavy with expectation, yet fragile with anticipation, not quite daring to dream any more than I am.

I'll go to bed tonight because it's time for that sort of thing, and in the morning I'll check off all the boxes that make up my day. All of my days. Days that threaten to stretch out before me, causing me to shudder at the mere thought of them. I'm unable to think about how many have already been stacked one on top of another, teetering and threatening to fall.

The happiness I once felt so strongly has slowly seeped away, leaving behind the empty ache of not having you like before.

I dream in fits, nothing like my dreams used to be.

I'm no longer who I was. Why am I the only one who sees?

I ache.

I weep.

And I wait.

I wait.

I wait.

I wait.

Because the only cure for what separates us is time. I don't know the exact amount that is required of me, but I do know that every day I play out the charade that passes as my life is a day closer to being with you.

So I play.

Kayleigh finally let out the breath she had been holding. Watching so many emotions flit across her friend's face had been hard. When Becca wiped away a tear or two, she had to hold back a few of her own. And now she just had to ask, so she whispered, "Tell me what you think."

"You were wrong, you know?"

"Wrong about what? I meant every word. Seriously. I was missing Robert so much the night I wrote that. I had already gone to bed and had to get back up just to write it all down."

Becca reached over and held her best friend's hand as she explained, "Not about the words. You were wrong about your writing. Kayleigh, it's the most beautiful poem you've ever written. Truly."

Smiling instead of answering, Kayleigh squeezed Becca's hand as she let thoughts of Robert wash over her. Yes, she had a huge puzzle to figure out, but no matter what she learned about her husband and his past, she knew their love had been real.

When her friend told her she had to leave, she knew she wouldn't have to deal with the loneliness that usually overtook her when she was by herself. She was actually looking forward to spending the night with memories of the love of her life. And she hoped for another dream. Maybe in this one she would finally learn the whole truth.

*

Becca was on the phone with her mother before she had backed out of Kayleigh's driveway. She was so glad she had someone to call when she needed help. Her mother had, over the years, somehow become a true friend, someone she could ask for advice without receiving any judgement.

"Mom, I'm worried about Kayleigh. I read part of her journal tonight. Don't worry; it was with her permission. What she wrote was a little dark. It bothered me, but I didn't want to show her how I was feeling."

"Explain what you mean by dark."

"It was the most emotional thing I've ever read. She's just in so much pain, Mom. It wasn't scary or anything. I don't think she's in any danger, but I'm not sure her head's in the right place."

"How was she when you left her?"

"That's the weird thing. She seemed better than I've seen her in a long time. She allowed me to read the journal, and she didn't mind that I basically saw into her head, but that's normal for best friends, right? She didn't make excuses about how dark it was. I guess that's what's bothering me."

"I think the best thing you can do right now is to pray for her. And check up on her. Maybe give her a call when you get home. Text her in the morning. Just be her friend. Becca, just

keep treating her like you have been."

Chapter Thirty-One

Kayleigh was glad Becca was gone. She hadn't exactly wanted to share her innermost feelings, even with her best friend who knew her better than anyone. Shaking her head sadly, she now realized how true that was. Robert had known everything about her, but he was gone, so Becca really did know her best now, especially after tonight. She could only imagine what her friend was thinking as she was driving home. Leaving her journal out in the open had been a dumb move. She had let the words pour out of her the other night, and now they were more than just her thoughts, now they were something she was going to have to deal with. And she had no one to blame but herself.

Even though she knew it was going to hurt, probably even more than it did when she first wrote the words, she knew she had to read her journal before going to bed. Maybe if she read enough about what was going on inside her own heart, she would figure out what her husband had wanted her to know.

She knew she was setting herself up for another night of dreams, and maybe even nightmares, but she had to get to the end of this story. She didn't want to let Robert go and, deep in her heart, she knew she never would, but she also knew she had to move forward more than she had so far. So she opened the book and sat down to read.

*

Sweat caused her pink flannel nightgown to stick to her body, but Kayleigh barely noticed the discomfort. She didn't need to look at her bedside clock to know it was the middle of the night. She could tell she had only been asleep a few hours even though she felt like she had slept for days. She wasn't the least bit tired, so she got up. Thinking that it might help if she wrote about this dream before too much time passed, she went downstairs and sat at her puzzle table. Grabbing a piece of paper and a pen, she wrote so quickly that her words came out looking more like scribbles than anything else, but she knew she would have no trouble translating it all later. What was important now was to get it out of her head and onto paper, so she wrote.

This dream had been confusing. Robert had read her journal and wept. She had been standing behind him, reading it over his shoulders when she had felt tremors make their way off his body as his soft cries had turned into sobs. It had hurt her to feel his pain, but she knew he had to experience it in order to get some relief, so she didn't try to comfort him. He had never turned around, never acknowledged her. She hadn't even cared in the dream that she didn't see his face, but now that she was awake she was desperate for even a shadowy memory of it. She knew now, more than ever, that she had no control over her dreams. They were just slices of memories coming together at different times in a very confusing way. Determined to make some sense out of them, she continued to write.

After Robert had finished reading her journal, the dream had shifted. She was no longer in their home with him. She was back at his house, the one he had grown up in. Surprised at the look on her mother-in-law's face, she had desperately wanted to reach out to her to offer her a hug. She clearly needed to be comforted. No matter how close she got to the other woman, she never could reach her, so Kayleigh just stood still and watched. Watched as Sally Wilson slowly pulled herself together before picking up the phone. Even in her dream, she fell to her knees as she realized what the conversation was about. Robert's mom had called him. Judging by the questions she asked, this phone call had taken place after they had gotten married. Kayleigh could only assume she had heard part of this conversation in real life, and it had finally come back to her in the dream. Her husband, on the other end of the phone, had obviously been upset because his mom's body language screamed distress. She had confronted him about someone named Meghan, asking him if he knew anything about a baby. When she had held the phone out and stared at it, Kayleigh knew Robert had hung up, but she couldn't believe it. She had never known her husband to be a rude person, and she found it hard to believe he would ever have hung up on his own mother. But the dream was so real, and she knew her memories were too. Now she just had to figure out why her husband had gotten so upset at the mention of Meghan's name.

Chapter Thirty-Two

September 1992

Meghan hadn't wanted to move away, but she had listened to her parents. She didn't have the strength to stand up to them. They had seen how upset she was after Sarah's accident, so they had called her aunt and asked for a favor, but now she was home, and everything was so different. It felt like she had been gone a lot longer than a year, and it surprised her how, in some ways, she almost didn't recognize her own parents. A lot about their home wasn't the same. The bedroom where she had spent so many nights laughing with her sister now felt like a prison cell. Her dad barely looked at her and her mom was too busy to even notice her.

When school started back, Meghan got on the bus, went from class to class, and came home to do homework. Then she started it all over again the next day. No one tried to sit with her at lunch, and she never had plans on the weekends. She felt like her life was a waiting game. Somehow she convinced herself if she could survive until graduation, then she could move away to college and never come back. Her parents definitely had plenty to occupy them now, and neither one seemed to want to talk about Sarah, so she gave them what they wanted. Retreating to her room night after night, she put on her headphones to drown out the sounds of her family. She knew she was creating distance between them, but she couldn't help it. Just looking at their faces the few minutes a day she was required to sit at the dinner table with them was more than she could take. Too many memories staring back at her caused her to sink further and further into a depression that scared her. The one person who would understand was gone, would always be gone. Meghan didn't know what to do, so she did nothing.

*

August 2016

Kayleigh hated to bother Chief at the station again, but he was the only person who could help her. She waited until her lunch break before walking the few blocks to the place her husband had spent so much of his time. If only she was surprising him with lunch. If only he would be waiting for her when she walked through the station door. But she knew it was useless to let herself get lost in those fantasies. Gone were the days of feeling her breath catch when she caught a glimpse of her husband in his bunker gear. No, when she walked into the station today, there would be familiar faces, but none of them would light up with a smile just for her.

Opening the door a few minutes later, she went straight to the office of her husband's oldest friend. Seeing that it was open, she leaned her head in and softly cleared her throat to get the attention of the man bent over a pile of papers.

"Kayleigh Wilson, so good to see you." The broad smile that instantly covered his face made her smile too. Chief was such a kind person. She was certain he would help her if he could.

Sitting down in the chair he pulled out for her, Kayleigh didn't waste any time before saying, "I need some help."

"Anything you need. Anything at all. Just ask."

"It's about Robert and Meghan." As soon as she said this, she noticed Chief's face got just a little bit pale. Knowing she had struck a nerve, she continued, "I keep remembering things, but you know that. I have these dreams where bits and pieces of the past come to me. Well, I've been writing them down, and somehow this girl Meghan is at the root of it all."

"Kayleigh, it might be best to leave the past buried, you know?"

"So there is more. Please, just tell me."

"I don't know if what I'm about to tell you will bring you any peace. Are you sure you want to know?"

"I have to be honest with you. At first, I was comforted by the dreams, and then it got a little weird. I'm finally at the place where I think Robert would want me to know whatever it is in his past that he was hiding. Don't get me wrong. I don't think he's actually reaching out to me or anything like that. I know it's just tiny memories coming to the surface, and I'm sure my grief has caused it all. But if he were still here, and if I asked him who Meghan was? Well, yeah, I think he would tell me.

That doesn't explain why he kept it a secret, but maybe he was planning to tell me. In fact, if I'm being totally honest now, there were several times he tried to open up about something. What if it was this? So, yes, I really want to know."

Sighing as he ran his hand over his face, Chief attempted a smile before saying, "I'll tell you everything I know, but I honestly don't think it's going to satisfy you. You see, Robbie dated Sarah back in high school, but he really liked her little sister Meghan. It was unheard of, and he was a little ashamed of it all. I've told you some of this, but there's more. This is the part that's going to be really hard for you to hear, okay?" Waiting until Kayleigh nodded for him to go on, Chief continued, "There's just no easy way to say this. You see, Meghan got pregnant, and she never told Robert. She confided in her sister, but she waited until after the abortion. That's what Sarah came over to tell him the night she died in the accident. Poor Robbie never forgave himself for any of it."

Kayleigh had started crying as soon as she heard the words that told her Robert had been a father. She looked into Chief's eyes as she said, "So he could have children? It was always me?"

Chief didn't know how to answer, so he just offered a sad smile as he gently went on, "That's all I know. We left for college right after graduation. That was only a couple of months after Sarah died. Robbie never really wanted to go home on breaks. He never tried to reach out to Meghan which always bothered him, but he was so afraid his parents would find out. And then, of course, he met you. He loved you so much, you have to know that. I think he wanted to tell you all of this, but part of him was afraid he would lose you. In a lot of ways he was tormented. I never knew exactly how to help him, and I'd be lying if I said I don't feel guilty. I let my best friend down, and it's too late to tell him I'm sorry."

"Chief, do you think that's it? Is that all he was trying to tell me? I mean, it's shocking, and I can certainly see how he was ashamed and all, but it just feels like there's more to it all."

"I promise you that's all I know. If there was something else, he never told me. I know it just about killed him when you guys never had a baby. He didn't know how to tell you that he already knew he could, you know? It was like he had somehow caused it by not being there for Meghan. I think he felt responsible for her getting an abortion even though she never even told him she was pregnant. It was all such a mess back then. The night Sarah died was just awful, and Robbie died thinking he had caused her death."

Kayleigh stood up and walked toward the door. Putting her hand on the doorknob, Chief felt something squeeze in his chest. The last time he had seen Robbie do the exact same thing was when he had broken the news to him about working with the rookie. Thinking about Trent Jefferson reminded him that there was actually one more thing he could tell Kayleigh. He quickly decided there was no need to tell her the connection. After all, Meghan's little brother couldn't help Kayleigh Wilson deal with any of her pain.

"Bye Chief. Thanks so much for telling me."

Getting up from his chair, he quickly made it to the door and spun her around. Giving her a long hug, he whispered in her ear, "Please don't think he didn't love you. I think it was his love for you that made him keep all of this a secret. I'm so sorry. About everything."

Hugging him back, Kayleigh tried to agree. Her tears were blocking her voice from telling him what she needed to say, so she squeezed him one last time before leaving his office. She was glad she had asked, shocked at what she had learned, and absolutely heartbroken to know she had cost her husband the joy of becoming a father. It was a lot to process, so she sent her boss a quick text explaining that she was taking the afternoon off. She needed to go home to be alone with her thoughts and her feelings. There was a lot of both to sort through.

Chapter Thirty-Three

2012

Robert forced himself to hang the phone up gently. He was all too aware of how intensely Kayleigh was watching him. He had tried to keep the edge out of his voice as he listened to his mother telling him all about the part of his past he wished she had never learned about. He knew his wife had heard bits and pieces, and he could only hope she would choose not to question him. Up until now, his only lies had been those of omission, but he knew if she asked him about the conversation, he would do more than hold back the truth from her. This fact, even if only admitted to himself, made him feel like a terrible husband. He certainly wasn't the man his wife deserved. Wiping the sweat from his face with his hand before he turned around, he wished he could wipe his shame away as easily.

"That sounded serious. Are your parents okay?"

Grateful when she gave him an easy out, Robert couldn't ignore the instant cramping he felt in his gut as he opened his mouth to spin the truth, "Mom's just worked up about Dad. I guess when you've been married as long as they have you start to get on each other's nerves. That won't happen with us though, right?"

Kayleigh leaned into the hug her husband was offering her. She knew he would think she was silly if he knew, but she loved his hugs as much for his smell as the feel of his arms around her. The man smelled amazing, and she loved every chance she got to breathe in the scent that was unique to him. Despite buying him cologne the first several years they were together, she never could get him to use any of it. Now that they were older, she was glad. There was so much about her husband that she found attractive, so she guessed she shouldn't be surprised that she liked the way he smelled. She giggled as she thought about where her mind had travelled.

Pulling away, Robert bent down to leave a gentle kiss on his wife's mouth before asking, "Care to tell me what's so funny, Mrs. Wilson?"

"Mr. Wilson, wouldn't you like to know?"

Grabbing his wife's hand and pulling her down on the couch with him, Robert breathed a silent sigh of relief. Knowing he could easily sell Kayleigh on the idea of a movie, he said, "Wanna go pop us some popcorn while I pick out a movie for us to watch?"

Jumping up from the couch and quickly heading to the kitchen, she called over her shoulder, "My vote is for a rom-com."

Even though they weren't his usual choice, he would happily watch any movie she chose tonight. Flipping through the binder that held only a small part of their large selection of DVDs, Robert held back a groan as he looked at his choices. He picked out three and waited for his wife to return to the couch with their bowls of popcorn.

"Almost ready! Do you have the movie choices ready for me?"

"You know I do."

Returning to the couch, Kayleigh glanced at the titles her husband had picked out. Raising an eyebrow at him, she asked,

"What's up? You picked three of my favorites. Hmmm…are you trying to butter me up or something?"

"No dear. The only thing I want to butter up is this popcorn. Just pick the show you want. I'm ready to snuggle up with you and watch the girl fall for the wrong guy before she figures out the other guy is the right guy. And then they kiss, right?"

Putting the DVDs back on the table, Kayleigh spun toward her husband as she said, "Oh wow! That reminds me of something. I had the most amazing dream last night." Pausing a moment, she grabbed both of his hands in her own before continuing, "It was so real. You and I were somewhere doing something. That parts a little fuzzy."

Robert squeezed her hands as he laughed a little. "Somewhere doing something? Nah, that's not fuzzy at all. Crystal clear. Go on though. Sorry I stopped your train of thought."

Lost in serious thought, Kayleigh didn't seem to catch the humor in his voice. "You put your arms around me and hugged me. It was the kind of hug that goes on and on. You kissed me too, but it's the hug I remember. Robert, this is gonna sound weird, but when I woke up this morning, I could still feel that hug. It felt so good, but it was more than that. It was like we hadn't seen each other in such a long time, and I woke up happy and unbelievably sad at the same time. It's like I knew it wasn't real, and that I would never hug you again."

"Kayleigh, you'll be getting hugs from me when we're old and grey. We'll be the talk of the nursing home."

"Honey, I'm not kidding. I've never had a dream like that before. I know you weren't in bed with me when I woke up this morning, but how did I forget it? I've never had a dream so real before. Do you think it meant anything?"

"Actually no. I think my side of the bed was empty, so you missed me last night. But I'm more than happy to hug you now. Pick out a movie and let's get under this blanket."

Giggling a little, Kayleigh picked out what she wanted to watch and popped it into the machine. She pretended to watch it while they ate popcorn and snuggled under the blanket like usual. But her mind was somewhere else. She was back in the dream unable to escape the uneasy feeling trying to wash over her.

*

September 2016

Pick up, pick up, pick up. Kayleigh wasn't usually so impatient, but she needed to talk to Becca now. When she heard her friend's voicemail message, she hung up. She would hunt the woman down if she had to. Grabbing her car keys, she was out the door and in her car within a few seconds. It didn't take her long to drive the short distance between their houses, and when she saw her friend's small yellow car in the driveway, she let out the breath she hadn't know she was holding.

Knocking on the door with all her might, Kayleigh almost fell into her friend's house a few seconds later. Becca laughed as she held the door with one hand and reached out to steady her friend with the other.

"Becca, I remembered something."

All laughter gone from her voice, she pulled her friend into the house before saying, "Let's go sit on the couch. Can I get you anything to drink?"

Not appearing to hear her friend's offer, Kayleigh said, "I had a dream when Robert and I were married. I remember telling him about it, but he brushed me off. Becca, in the dream I felt Robert the same way I feel him now. I didn't understand it at the time, and I don't really understand it now, but it has to mean something, right?"

"I guess. Look, I'm guessing you've always been a big dreamer, but you just never had a reason to remember them. If I had to say, you had these dreams as a little girl too. It's a wonderful gift for sure. I still think you're dreaming about memories you've hidden from yourself all these years. I don't think you realized at the time that you were seeing or hearing things that were important, but now your brain is trying to make sense of so much. Man, it's exhausting, isn't it?"

"Yes, that's a perfect word for it. I'm more than just tired. My brain hurts. My body aches. And I'm not exactly refreshed when I wake up in the morning. I'm ready for it all to stop. How do I make the dreams stop?"

Becca put her arms around her friend and pulled her into a gentle hug before saying, "When you put all the pieces together, all the memories, then I think this will stop. I think the way Robert died has something to do with it too. Do you ever wonder about how it was declared an accident, but you still don't know what really happened? Kayleigh, I think the way you don't really know what happened that night is part of these dreams. You need closure on all of it."

Wiping away the tears that started falling as soon as Becca started holding her, Kayleigh said, "Yeah, I need to figure it all out."

"No, you're never going to figure it out. But I do believe it will all come to you one day. Just be patient, okay? But keep coming to me too, okay? It's so much lighter when we share the burdens of this life with those we love."

Pulling out of the hug, Kayleigh thanked her before asking

for a cup of tea. Eager to change the subject, she added, "And some cookies?"

"Girl, don't you know I'm on a diet? That's not to say I don't have a stash of cookies. You know I do. Come on into the kitchen with me."

They didn't mention Robert anymore, but he was never far from either of their minds. Becca watched her friend carefully while Kayleigh pretended not to notice. Long after she went home and Becca had climbed into bed, their conversation seemed to still be floating around the house. Closing her eyes, she prayed for her friend. She prayed for peace, but she also prayed for closure. She hadn't missed the near-panicked look in Kayleigh's eyes. It worried her. She wasn't sure how much longer this could go on.

Chapter Thirty-Four

Sitting at the puzzle table was making Kayleigh's back ache, but she was determined to see what was hiding right in front of her. Deciding to put the dreams in chronological order, she started shifting around the pieces of paper hoping to see a pattern. As she read everything she had written down, she let her mind drift back to what it had been like to be Robert's wife. He had made her feel so comfortable, so secure, so wanted. She thought about spending the night wrapped in his arms and also about the nights she slept alone while he was at work. It surprised her that she couldn't remember having a single nightmare during their marriage. She had known the danger involved in her husband's line of work, but somehow she hadn't given into the fear of what could exactly happen during a fire. She credited Robert for giving her peace of mind back then. She only wished she could be as strong now without him. She'd give anything for the dreams to run their course, but more than that, she needed to find out why she had started having them in the first place.

Reading about the car accident again sent chills down Kayleigh's arms. What was it about this particular dream that bothered her so much? And why did it make her think of Sally Wilson. There was a missing piece that she just couldn't put her finger on.

Standing up, Kayleigh walked toward the bookcase. Maybe if she looked at some old photo albums she would find a picture or two of Robert's mom that would jar something loose in her mind. Oh, how she missed his parents. Missed seeing the way Robert instantly became a little boy again when he walked into his childhood home.

When she found the picture of Robert in the kitchen with his mom, the one where sunlight had bathed them in so much beauty, she remembered how she had immediately grabbed the family camera to capture the perfect shot. And what a beautiful photo it had turned out to be. The love between the two of them had never seemed as real as it had that day. Until the dream. Kayleigh gasped as she realized she was looking at the same expression on her mother-in-law's face as the one from the dream.

After that, more pieces started to fall into place. Thinking about Robert and his mom made her remember the days spent baking cookies and looking at the boxes of mementos from his childhood. She was sure Miss Corbett had been mentioned somewhere along the way. Robert's mom had been the kind to save stuff, and Kayleigh could almost remember seeing stacks of homemade crafts from when her husband had been a little boy. She shook her head slightly. She couldn't believe she had somehow buried all these memories.

Looking at the rest of the slips of papers, she wondered when she would remember everything else. But for the first time in a long time, she felt a sense of peace. No, she didn't know the answer to whatever this mystery was, but she had hope. And hope was something she was grateful to have. She was learning a little more every day to be grateful for what she did have instead of focusing on what had been taken from her.

*

September 1992

Meghan was glad to be back home. Her aunt's house had been stuffy and boring. At first, it had been exactly what she had needed, but once those first few months had relieved her of her pain and so much more, she had wondered around feeling lost. Finally, she had asked her parents if she could come home. They convinced her to wait until the end of the summer, hoping that the new school year would be the distraction their daughter needed. Being at home wasn't a good idea for her even if they didn't quite know how to explain it so she would understand.

Grateful to be back in her old room, Meghan tried not to think about how much her life had changed in such a short amount of time. She was sure she would look back one day and understand why it all had to happen, but she wished she had someone to talk to about it now. Her mom was too busy and her dad didn't seem to see her anymore, so she lived among them if not really with them. It was strange to not feel like she was a part of her own family, but that's exactly what her life was like now. And the worst part was knowing it was all her fault. No one could convince her that Sarah's accident hadn't been caused by her. She knew deep in her heart that her sister would have paid better attention to her driving if she hadn't been so worried. Meghan knew she had been the last thing on Sarah's mind right before she died. She couldn't explain how she knew it, but she did. It haunted her every night and stayed in her mind every day. Sometimes it felt like more than she could bear, but she went on. She had told Sarah one time that they would go to college together, both destined to be world-famous journalists. She didn't care about the fame anymore, but she was determined to learn to write for her sister. She had a story to tell and the perfect person to dedicate it to.

Chapter Thirty-Five

November 2016

Becca liked the spring she saw in her friend's step. Kayleigh looked lighter somehow as she walked the short distance from the coffee shop parking lot to the table in the window. She seemed more like herself, no longer looking like the tired version Becca had been so worried about.

"Well, hey you. It seems like forever since we've met here for coffee."

"And scones. Please don't forget the chocolate and pecan scones." Smiling down at her friend, Kayleigh walked to the counter to place their orders, quickly slipping back into their old routine. With her back to their table, she didn't see the relieved smile on Becca's face.

Walking back to the table while balancing the plate with their treats on it and two cups of coffee, Kayleigh felt an overwhelming sense of normalcy wash over her. She knew they would eventually talk about Robert today, but it didn't fill her with despair like it had just a few weeks ago. She smiled as she thought about how her husband would gently punch her on her shoulder if he was here, his way of letting her know he was proud of her. She was proud of herself too.

"So, tell me what has you breezing in here like that. You look happier than I've seen since, well, since forever."

"You can say it, Becca. Since Robert died. Yeah, I'm starting to feel a little healed, and it feels good."

"I'm glad. You deserve to be happy. He would want that too. You know that, right?"

"I actually have been realizing that more and more lately. I've also been making sense out of my dreams and memories and all that. I think I've figured a few things out."

As the two friends talked while munching on one of their favorite treats, Kayleigh's face suddenly got pale. Alarmed, Becca said, "You feeling okay? You don't look so good all of a sudden."

"I just remembered something. This is the table. The table where Robert sat with that woman. I remember seeing them, but he had told me he had a meeting, so I wasn't too alarmed. I can't remember exactly who he had said she was, but since my dream, I've remembered the look on his face. He was scared that day."

"Scared? Are you sure? Why would he be scared?"

"I have no idea. All I know is I remember asking him about her. He must have given me the answer I wanted to hear because I don't remember being jealous or suspicious or anything like that."

"Well, that does sound like you. I can't remember you ever being the jealous type. But why would you be? Robert never had eyes for anyone but you. I loved to watch him looking at you. His love was so strong; you felt like you could reach out and touch it."

"I loved him like that too. Look, Becca, there's something I need to talk to you about. I've sort of made my peace with it, but I'd be lying if I said it doesn't keep me up at nights. I confronted Chief and learned something."

"Right, you told me about the girl Robert dated a bit. The one who died in a car accident, right? Tragic."

"I wish that was all. I don't mean it like that sounded. I hate that a young girl died, and I feel so bad Robert kept it from me, but it's something much bigger."

Becca sipped what was left of her coffee as she waited for her friend to continue. The lightness had certainly left her face, a sure sign that she was struggling with what she was about to share.

Taking a deep breath, Kayleigh said, "There was another girl. Actually, she was the first girl's sister. Now, I don't know how to say this without making Robert look bad, so please remember how young he was. Teenagers are dumb in general, right? And he was a teen boy, so there's that. Anyway, he got this girl pregnant." Kayleigh paused, knowing Becca would need a minute to process what she had just heard. Continuing, she said, "I think that's what was going on when Robert would just stare into space."

Breaking her silence, Becca asked, "You went back to see Chief again?"

"I did. He was very reluctant to tell me, but he finally shared it all. Or at least I think he did. I can't imagine there could be anything else."

"I can't believe you didn't tell me. Kayleigh, all those years you two tried to have a baby, Robert knew all along that it wasn't him? Honey, are you mad at him?"

"I was. I was furious in fact. Then I put myself in his shoes. Sometimes in a marriage there's a lot that goes unsaid. I never really shared with him what my childhood was like. I just couldn't. And he understood, never pushing me to tell him or asking a lot of questions. We always danced around it, but not in an awkward way. We were just careful to not talk about it. I kind of think that's where his head was at with this. It must have been such a heavy burden. I feel so bad he didn't let me help him carry it."

"I hate to ask, but the baby?"

"No, there wasn't a baby."

"Oh no. That must have tormented him. I know how strong his faith was though. And he always talked about how he didn't start following Jesus until college. A lot of things are making sense for you now, aren't they?"

"Not everything though. I can't get that woman out of my mind. This is going to sound crazy, but what if it was her?"

"His old girlfriend? Why would he have met with her?"

Pushing the crumbs around the plate with her finger, Kayleigh sighed as she said, "I don't know. My mind is on overdrive I guess."

"Let's go. I think we need to walk around and get some fresh air. You've given me a lot to think about."

"Thanks for everything. Becca, I sure do love you."

"Right back at ya."

Chapter Thirty-Six

November 1992

Meghan missed her best friend. School wasn't the same without someone to share it all with. She went through the motions, spending her days trying to avoid everyone she knew. She just didn't feel like hanging out anymore. Everyone got so awkward around her because of Sarah. If only they knew everything. She could only imagine the way they would stare if they truly knew it all, so she kept to herself. She wished school was her only problem, but what waited for her at home was so much worse. Every night all she could think about was going back to school to do it all over again.

Her dad never looked at her anymore, and she knew she was to blame. Her mom was too busy to even think about her, but she had to wonder what she thought about late at night after they all had gone to bed. She often heard sounds from the kitchen long after everyone else was tucked away for the night. Knowing it was best to not interrupt her mom's one chance at solitude, it took everything in her not to tiptoe downstairs, sit on a bar stool like she used to do, and tell her everything that was bothering her. Like so much from her childhood, those days were long gone. And she had no one to blame but herself.

Crying into her pillow, she started thinking about Sarah and where she would be now if all of this hadn't happened. When Robbie entered her thoughts, she pulled out her headphones and cranked up her music. Anything to get thoughts of him out of her head. She knew she just had to get through high school, move away to college, and never ever come back home. Maybe one day she could truly leave everything in her past. She knew she would do it for Sarah. She would get the scholarship they had always talked about, take journalism classes, and then travel the world, covering important stories. Every single one would be dedicated to her sister, even if no one ever knew.

Rolling over in bed, Meghan removed her headphones and prayed for sleep to come. When the crying started like it did most nights, she put her hands over her ears. Why did she have to live with the reminder of the worst time in her life? She knew

time would work its way and the crying would eventually stop,

but that didn't stop her from counting the days until she never

had to be reminded of its source again.

*

November 2016

Chief felt sick to his stomach. He hated that Kayleigh had

pushed him so hard, but he hadn't been able to keep the truth

from her. He wondered what Robbie would think of him. He

had managed to keep his promise for so many years, decades

even. And in one moment of weakness, he had told Kayleigh

everything. He hadn't been able to call her to see how she was

doing, but he really didn't need to. He knew she had to be a

mess. All those years of trying to have children. He had never

understood how his friend had kept the secret when he knew

how much pain his wife was in. Man, it had to have been agony

for Robbie, but it had obviously been more important to save

face. For the first time in a long time, he felt like punching his

best friend in the face. He knew the accident had been just that, but what if telling the truth years ago could have softened Kayleigh's heart toward adoption? Wiping a hand over his eyes, Chief wished things were different. A son or a daughter would certainly be able to offer Kayleigh comfort in a way no one else could, but Robbie had robbed her of that, and he had helped. It made him sick to think about it all.

*

Kayleigh couldn't get Meghan out of her mind. How she wished Robert's mom was still alive. She wondered if his parents had known their son had gotten a girl pregnant. She doubted it. They had longed for a grandchild even though their kindness had kept them from mentioning it too often. Kayleigh hadn't missed the look that would enter her mother-in-law's eyes when they were out shopping together. If a young mother was close by with a child in a stroller, Sally Wilson would get this faraway look in her eyes. Kayleigh had even seen her brush away a tear or two, but she always acted like she didn't notice. Not that she didn't care, she did, but she also knew exactly how the other woman felt. It broke her heart too to see what she couldn't have.

But now she wondered if those looks might have been something else. Maybe Robert's mom had been grieving the grandchild she lost. Had she known about the abortion? Kayleigh couldn't imagine the pain of knowing you had lost your grandchild in such a senseless way. She personally couldn't wrap her head around the man she had loved for so long being involved in something like that. Robert had loved everyone and had fought hard at his job to keep people alive. He had put his life on the line time and time again to save others. No, it didn't make any sense that he would have agreed to an abortion.

Kayleigh picked up her cup of tea and walked from the kitchen to the puzzle table that had slowly become a command center for what she called now her Robert Project. She knew she wouldn't rest until she could put all of this behind her, not that she ever would actually get over any of it, but now she had a new piece to the puzzle. Finding Meghan seemed impossible, but she had a plan. When she had called Chief about meeting for coffee in the morning, she had felt a little guilty. She was about to ask him to betray his best friend, and she prayed she could talk him into it. Being this way didn't bring her any pleasure, but she was past the point of caring. Nothing would stand in the way of her getting the answers she was so desperate for.

Chapter Thirty-Seven

When he heard the clicking of high heels steadily making their way toward his office, Chief knew who it was. Kayleigh was nothing if she wasn't punctual, so he didn't need to look at the clock to know it was exactly 8:00. He sighed deeply as he pushed off from his desk to lift himself up. The pounds he had allowed to creep on felt heavier today somehow. He knew it was dread weighing him down more than the number that had stared back at him from his bathroom scales this morning. He already knew what Robbie's widow wanted to know. He didn't need her to ask, but he would let her. He could kick himself for letting her get the truth out of him, but it was too late to reel it back in now.

Opening the door at the exact moment he heard her footsteps pause, he reached forward to hug her. When he felt the way her body stiffened a bit at his touch, he wondered why. Was she as nervous as he was, or was part of her mad at him for his role in the deception that had been forced upon her for so long? He could understand both feelings, so he let go of her without mentioning the lack of a response on her part.

"Do you want to sit in my office and talk, or would you prefer going to a coffee shop?"

Hearing the resignation in his voice softened Kayleigh's heart. Smiling at him, she answered, "Let's go out. I don't really want to talk about this here, you know? There's too much of Robert here."

Grabbing his jacket, Chief shoved his arms into the sleeves before reaching into his front pocket for his keys. "Want me to drive us?"

"How about I just meet you there? Let's go to that coffee shop on James Street. You know the one?"

Chief smiled a genuine smile as he said, "Oh yes. Your husband made me drink many a cup of coffee from there. I'll see you there in a few."

Pulling into a parking space a few minutes later, Chief breathed in a deep breath. If he had to guess, things were about to get a lot worse for Kayleigh. He suspected she was about to ask him for more information about Meghan, and he knew he was about to rock her world with his answers. He just hoped it wouldn't be more than she could handle.

*

December 1992

"Mom? I know you're busy, but we need to talk."

Looking up from the pile of laundry she was folding, Karen Jefferson couldn't deny the desperation she saw in her daughter's eyes. Pushing aside the laundry to make room on the couch so they could both sit down, she sighed as she realized how she had allowed so much space to come between them. "Honey, sit down here with me." Putting her arm around this young woman who still reminded her of a little girl, she gave her a soft kiss on her cheek before asking, "What do you need to talk to me about?"

When she saw tears pool in Meghan's eyes, she resisted the urge to comfort her. If being a mother all these years had taught her nothing else, she knew silence was the best strategy to use right now.

"Mom, this is a lot harder than I thought it would be. The truth is I don't think I can live here anymore. Please let me move back in with Aunt Linda."

Trying to hide her shock at her daughter's words, she gently told her, "I'm sure your aunt would love to have you come back, and I promise to consider it too, but you need to understand something. Moving away isn't going to make all your problems disappear. I know this is about more than Sarah, but you have to think about Trent too."

"Mom, I just can't."

"I'm glad you wanted to talk. I've been wanting to talk to you too. You know Trent's getting old enough now to notice how you treat him. Honey, you just have to start paying attention to him. None of this is his fault, you know?"

"This has nothing to do with him. I just can't take it anymore. School is so useless. I don't even have any friends. All I want is to move away, get through high school, and go off to college. Sarah and I always talked about going together.

We were going to be journalists who travelled the world together. But I really messed it all up, didn't I?"

"You definitely made mistakes, but nothing we can't handle together. I know it seems like yours were bigger than most, but we all make them. I never went through anything like this when I was your age, but I certainly made my share of mistakes. I don't think running away is the answer, but I promise to think about it."

"Thanks. And I promise to try with Trent."

"You know I understand, right?"

"I do. I'll let you get back to your laundry. Man, it never seems to end, does it?"

"You have no idea. Trent goes through more clothes than you and your sister ever did. A little boy sure is different."

Wanting to smile at her mother, Meghan was sure what crossed her face looked more like a grimace. "I love you, Mom. I know I don't say it nearly enough, but I appreciate everything you're doing for me."

Watching her daughter walk away, Karen felt the all-too-familiar tightness in her chest again. If anyone had told her just a few years ago that her life would look like this, she would have laughed out loud. She had thought her child-rearing years were almost over, but then Trent had come into their lives. She loved him fiercely, but even she couldn't deny the tension he had brought to their household.

Thinking about Trent made her think about the time. She had less than an hour before he woke up from his nap, and once that happened all thoughts of folding laundry would become a memory. The child demanded all of her time, but she didn't have the heart to ask Meghan to help take care of him. Not yet anyway.

*

November 2016

"One vanilla latte for you and one cup of joe for me." Chief sat down across from Kayleigh and waited for her to open up to him. He was prepared to tell her whatever she needed to know, but he didn't want to be the one to bring it up first.

"Thanks so much. These are my favorite. Robert used to tease me all the time about my lack of coffee-drinking skills. He said there was so much sugar and flavoring in these things that they didn't deserve to be sold in a coffee shop. He never understood my love of tea either."

Laughing softly, Chief said, "I can't say I don't agree with him about the latte. Why does there have to be all that whipped topping on it?"

"I know! It's ridiculous, but have you ever tasted one? Totally worth all the fat and calories."

As they both sipped their drinks in silence for a few minutes, Kayleigh could feel herself relax a bit. Opening her mouth to speak, she closed it again. Looking at Chief, she tried again, "I guess you know why I invited you here today. I need to know more about Meghan. I can't help but think she's the key to all of this. Do you remember much about her? Even her last name will help."

Chief took one look into her eyes and the innocence and expectancy he saw there was all it took. Choosing his words carefully, he said, "I know her last name. It's Jefferson, but there's more you need to know. You're gonna want to ask a ton of questions, but will you let me say it all before you do?"

Nodding her head, Kayleigh knew she was going to be taking mental notes throughout this talk. She could only hope she didn't hear anything that would make her more disappointed in her husband than she already was. She still loved Robert and always would, but she knew the man she was learning about wasn't completely the same one she had known for so long, and she was having to fight the way her feelings for him were getting all mixed up.

"Okay, here goes. Meghan and Sarah probably would have stayed in Robbie's past if Trent Jefferson hadn't applied for a job. As part of the hiring practice, I require these rookies to write a pretty intensive essay. When I read the one Trent wrote, it didn't take long to figure out who he was. When I told Robbie, well, let's just say it was rough. He didn't want any reminders of his past creeping in, but I made him take the kid under his wing. I don't think Trent ever knew there was a connection between Meghan and Robbie, but I couldn't help but think it would help heal the past if they worked together. I don't know if I was right or wrong, but I don't think it matters now. I mean, Robbie's gone, and Trent has moved on. I'm sorry I don't know more to tell you."

"So, Trent and Meghan are related? How?"

Chief looked her in the eyes as he carefully answered, "They have to be brother and sister. Sarah and Meghan were only a year apart, but I guess their parents decided to try again. Quite the age difference, but it happens, right?" Wincing as soon as he said it, he added, "I'm sorry. That wasn't very sensitive of me."

"No, it's okay. Really. This is actually really good news. I mean, you have Trent's contact information, right? That means I'm almost guaranteed to be able to get in touch with Meghan. Maybe she can tell me what I need to know to figure all this out."

"I hope so. How about I give you a call when I get back to the station. Trent's information is in his file. I'll give you all of it."

Reaching across the table to hold his hand for a minute, Kayleigh felt a bit of the tension leave her shoulders. Talking to Trent would be awkward, but it would be a breeze compared to what it would be like to talk to Meghan. Before long, she would know the truth. It was a promise she had to hold onto.

Chapter Thirty-Eight

"Becca, I can't quite bring myself to call Trent. I just feel like it might not end the way I want it to. What if it's a dead end?"

Putting her feet up on her coffee table, Becca carefully answered her friend, "Call him and then call Meghan as soon as possible. Maybe what she tells you will help you let go of the heaviness of all that's been going on. That will help you refocus on all the good stuff. And there is a lot of good stuff still. You know that, right?"

"I do. I really do. I still have my bad days but not as many as before. I feel lighter, you know?"

"So? You gonna call Trent tonight or what?"

"Ugh! Yeah, I'm hanging up with you and calling him. I'll be in touch, okay?"

"I'll be praying for you, my friend."

Kayleigh walked around the house a bit without putting her phone down. Doing her best to find something to distract her, she just couldn't get Becca's voice out of her head. Letting out a deep breath, she sat down on the edge of her bed and looked at her phone. She had memorized Trent's number as soon as Chief had given it to her, so all she had to do was push a few buttons. Managing to let out a laugh and what sounded like a cry at the same time, she dialed his number before she could change her mind.

"Hello?"

Not recognizing the deep voice on the other end even though she had talked to him several times over the past couple of years, Kayleigh asked, "Is this Trent Jefferson?"

"Yep, sure is. Can I help you?"

"This is Kayleigh Wilson. I'm Robert's wife."

"I know who you are."

When Trent didn't say anything else, Kayleigh went on, "I

don't really know how to ask you this, but I recently found out that my husband knew your sister when they were younger. I would love to talk to her."

"My sister?"

"Yes, Meghan. I'm sorry. I should have been more sensitive. I'm so sorry about your sister Sarah, but I need to talk to Meghan. May I please have her number?"

"Um, yeah, I guess that would be okay, but I don't have it with me right now."

Thinking the conversation couldn't get more awkward, Kayleigh didn't question his response. She couldn't imagine a brother who didn't have his sister's phone number memorized. Unsure how to end the call, she said, "Sounds good. Do you mind getting in touch with me when you find it? I really want to talk to her as soon as possible."

"Sure thing. Uh, bye."

Staring at her phone, she couldn't quite believe the man had hung up on her. She needed to talk to someone who could help her with all of this, so she reached out to the only person who would understand. Calling Becca again, Kayleigh settled back on her bed to dissect the strange conversation with the young firefighter who had driven her husband crazy.

*

Trent couldn't breathe. How had things gotten so messy? When he had quit his job and moved out of town, he had honestly thought he had put his past behind him. He had no idea how to give Kayleigh Wilson what she wanted. His parents would be the ones to call to get Meghan's number, not him. How could he explain that to anyone, much less the widow of Robert Wilson?

He let the same thoughts that had plagued him for years circle around inside his head again. This was a moment in time he had felt so often before. That moment when he realized his memories, so lovingly cared for by him for so many years, weren't shared by who he thought they should be. He didn't understand how it was possible that times that meant so much to him, that had etched themselves deeply inside of him, weren't even remembered by the one person he had spent his life missing, the one person he needed to believe felt what he had, what he still felt. He wondered how a person can spend years reminiscing only to find out the other person in your memories not only doesn't share them with you but almost denies they even happened. The pain he felt was like losing something precious twice. Not only did he feel like the memory had suddenly been shredded in front of his eyes, but the love wrapped in it for so many years, when scratched past the surface, showed itself to be false. Now when the memory rose to the surface, he no longer met it with a smile. His smile just wasn't strong enough to penetrate the pain. And he was so very tired of feeling the pain.

Wiping at the tears that had fallen down his face onto his shirt, he couldn't stop where his thoughts were taking him. As much as he hated to do it, he couldn't stop remembering the moment when it all became so clear to him, when he couldn't believe he was just now. seeing it. How had his memories changed her face so much in his mind? The older he got, the more he remembered her unhappiness. And he would be lying if he said he didn't still want her in his life even as he remembered the hatred in her face staring at him. The look that was there all along, barely controlled under the surface. But he had a woman needing a phone number. And he needed all of this to end, so he picked up his phone and called the two people he hadn't talked to in years. The ones he had never planned to talk to again.

Chapter Thirty-Nine

Kayleigh couldn't wait for work to end. After her fourth major mistake, she had walked away from her desk. Needing to clear her mind, she went outside for a quick walk around her building. She was sure anyone glancing out the windows would wonder what she was doing, but she didn't care. She needed to get Robert and Meghan out of her mind, at least until she got home. For not the first time, she clenched her fists as thoughts of her husband keeping this secret from her washed over her. She wished she knew why he felt he needed to hide it from her. It didn't sound like something the man she had known would do. There had to be more to his story, and maybe if she found out what that was then she could forgive him.

Thinking through every possible scenario, she was surprised at where her thoughts kept returning. She kept remembering mistakes she had made in their marriage, times she had neglected Robert, and every opportunity she had lost. If only she had listened to him. Maybe he hadn't opened his mouth and spoken actual words that she could hear, but he had most definitely tried to tell her something over and over. Now that she wasn't so focused on herself, she could clearly see the pain her husband had been in. It shamed her to think how she had failed him as his wife.

Not wanting her boss to send someone out to find her, she made her way back inside. As soon as she started hitting the keys on her computer, her brain started overthinking it all again. Deciding to give up, she pulled out her phone to check for any missing calls or texts. Seeing the missed call from Trent's number made her heart speed up a little. Knowing she would need to wait until after work to return his call but not wanting to, she went to her boss's office to beg off work.

She didn't wait until she got into her car to call Trent back. Unlike the other day when it took more strength than she could have imagined to reach out to him, she was excited to make this call.

"Trent here."

"Yes, Trent? This is Kayleigh Wilson again. I missed your

call."

"I have Meghan's number for you. Do you have a pen?"

Within seconds she had pulled a pen and an old receipt out of her purse. Jotting down the number, she said, "Thanks so much. Trent, I've been wanting to talk to you about Robert."

"Uh, I gotta go. Hope you find out what you need."

Kayleigh wondered where this guy had learned his phone etiquette. Did he think hanging up on people was the way to end a call? But she knew now was not the time to worry about that. She had the number of the woman who had most likely been her husband's first love. The woman who many years ago had taken a pregnancy test and, unlike the dozens Kayleigh had taken over the years, got the news that a new life was growing inside of her. As much as she didn't want to, she felt herself having to resist the blanket of jealousy threatening to cover her. She knew she needed to focus on the fact that both Robert and Meghan had been too young to handle any of it.

Knowing she couldn't call her right now, Kayleigh headed home. Maybe she could find a way to connect with her husband just a little bit before making the call she was dreading. She had to draw strength from somewhere.

Pulling into her driveway a few minutes later, Kayleigh just sat in her car. Closing her eyes, she started praying. Asking God for help was as natural to her as breathing, but lately she had been so caught up with her Robert Project that she had neglected to reach out to the One who loved her more than her husband ever could have. Praying until she felt the gentle release of peace that always came over her when she knew it was time to say amen, she opened the car door and let it shut softly behind her.

As she entered her home, she knew in her heart that it wasn't quite time to make the phone call to Meghan. She still felt the need to somehow be with her husband first. Glancing around each room as she walked through them, some photo albums on their bookcase caught her eye. It had been a few months since she had pulled them off the shelf, but she still knew which ones she wanted to look at.

Before long she was on the couch with her feet tucked under her, memories finding their way down her cheeks. Laughing at a picture of herself from their college days, she almost missed Robert in the background. She had forgotten about this day, and she couldn't remember the last time she had looked at this picture carefully. In fact, she couldn't honestly say she remembered ever noticing her husband in the picture at all. Something about the way he looked was familiar to her. He looked different somehow. No matter how hard she stared at his reflection, it just wouldn't come to her. Pulling the photo out of the album, she walked away from the couch to put it on the front of their refrigerator. Choosing the magnet from their trip to Pike's Peak, she let memories of happier times wash over her as she continued to stare at the picture.

Deciding she was letting distraction take over, she went back to the couch in search of her phone. Knowing it was time, she pulled the receipt with Meghan's phone number on it out of her pocket. Taking a deep breath as she dialed the number, she tried to calm the racing of her heart.

After the fourth ring, she was starting to feel a little bit like a stalker. Before she could decide whether to leave a message or not, she was surprised when she heard a soft voice on the other end say, "Hello?"

"Um, hello? Yes, this is Kayleigh Wilson. Is this Meghan Jefferson?"

"Yes. Who did you say you are again? I don't know anyone named Kayleigh."

Laughing more from nervousness than humor, she went on, "Oh, of course you don't. I'm sorry. I'm a bit nervous. Uh, Trent gave me your number."

"Trent?"

Kayleigh didn't miss the way the woman's voice changed. She couldn't be sure after hearing just one word, but it sounded like Meghan was afraid. Why would she be afraid of her own brother? She knew she needed to continue, so she added, "Your brother. He and my husband worked together. In fact, my husband is the reason I'm calling you."

"I'm sorry, but I'm confused. Who is your husband, and how do I know him?"

"Well, you knew him. My husband actually passed away recently. He had been working with Trent, and it's actually a very long story. Robert died in a fire, and after a lot of thinking I put some pieces together and they led me to you."

"Me?"

"You probably knew him as Robbie Wilson back then."

"Oh my, yes. I never thought I'd hear that name again."

"Look, do you think we could meet somewhere? I know the area code, so I know we're only a few hours apart. It sounds so weird, but can I meet you for coffee tomorrow? I'll gladly drive to you."

In a soft whisper, Meghan answered, "Of course. I'm so sorry about Robbie. I didn't know. Look, why don't we meet halfway?"

When plans had been made to meet for coffee, both women said an uncomfortable good-bye. Once she hung up, Kayleigh just sat and held the phone in her trembling hands. She couldn't believe she was going to collide with Robert's past

tomorrow. She hoped she could handle what she would learn.

Chapter Forty

Trent looked down at the weights he had been using to work on his biceps. He fought back the urge to pick one up and throw it at the wall. He knew the small bit of pleasure the act would bring him wasn't worth the hours it would take to repair the hole it would leave behind. He just couldn't get Meghan off his mind. He couldn't allow himself to think about Robert either. He knew if he spent too much time thinking about him, he would do a lot more than just think about throwing something through a wall. In fact, he was scared about what he would do if he let thoughts of Robert get too far into his mind.

But Meghan? He had never wanted to hear her name again. At least with Robert there had been a chance. Once he figured out that the other man saw him as both a pest and a responsibility, he had lost it. He didn't want to risk what would happen if he ever saw Meghan again.

He had spent years trying to get his sister to like him. Laughing as the word sister crossed his mind, Trent stood up from his weight bench. He needed a drink. He didn't care that it was still morning. He had to have something to dull the pain that was creeping over him. It seemed like he had spent his entire life trying to escape that feeling.

Knowing how the rest of his day was going to play out, he walked away from the weights and entered the kitchen. Not even bothering with a glass, he grabbed the bottle of Jack from the back of the cabinet and wiped off the dust that had gathered on it since the last time he pulled it out. He was trying hard, but days like today made him want to do whatever it took to get the pain to go away. And nothing brought the pain back into focus like Meghan did.

*

2001

Trent just wanted to stop hearing the screams that seemed to float up the stairs and into his bedroom night after night. He couldn't make out many words, but he knew his parents and sister were all mad about something. He kept hearing them talk about his sister Sarah who had died before he was born. His mom always stopped yelling and started crying every time her name was brought up. He knew it would stop soon because Meghan never stayed long when she came home for a visit. He had tried so many times to get her to play with him, but she didn't seem to want to look at him, much less sit at the table and play the games he set out for them. His mom always told him to keep trying, but it was getting so hard. He was starting to think they were all mad about him, but that didn't make any sense. His name came up a lot though, so he knew that had to mean something.

When he heard the front door slam shut, he rushed to his window to see who it was this time. Seeing his dad standing in their front yard with his hands on his knees, bent over like he was looking at the grass, made Trent want to call out to him. He hated seeing everyone in his family so sad. He wished he could do something to make it all go away.

*

Frozen in Time

November 2016

Trent held the near-empty bottle up to the light. He liked the way the whiskey tasted, the smooth burn he felt as it went down his throat, and especially the way it helped him forget about his problems. Propping his feet on his coffee table, he thought about calling his parents but let the thought leave as quickly as it had come. Talking to his mom the other day just long enough to ask for Meghan's number had been enough. He couldn't deny it had given him a small jolt of pleasure when he had heard the hurt in her voice. Good, she needed to hurt. He wanted her to feel at least a fraction of the pain she had caused him. No, he wouldn't be calling his parents again, not ever if he had anything to do with it. And he hoped whatever Kayleigh Wilson wanted with Meghan would crush her too. He couldn't believe how many years he had wasted on his family.

*

2001

"No, Mom, I won't play with him. How many times have I explained it to you? I can't stand to even look at him."

"Meghan, you're being cruel. Trent is just a boy, and he's been trying to get your attention his entire life. Ten years, Meghan! The poor boy has been trying to make you his friend for ten whole years. Don't you have any room in your heart for him?"

Refusing to give in even though she felt like she was being torn in half, she told her mom, "Look, I'm really sorry. I know you sacrificed so much for me, but I just can't change the way I feel. Could we please get through dinner tonight? I really want to come visit you and Dad, but I can't deal with all this drama."

Seeing the anguish in her daughter's eyes made her own fill with tears, but she held them back as she said, "Okay. Let's please try to enjoy our dinner. And at least smile at your brother, okay?"

Resisting the urge to roll her eyes, Meghan said, "Really, Mom?" Not waiting for an answer, she walked away. It had been a mistake to come home for the weekend, but she was good at learning from her mistakes. After tonight, her mom wouldn't have to worry about how she acted at the dinner table anymore.

*

November 2016

Trent didn't bother with the table. He let the bottle of Jack slide out of his hand and onto the floor. There wasn't enough left in it to drink anyway, and it seemed like a lot of effort to focus on making his hand reach all the way from the couch to the table. Hearing the loud thud as the bottle hit his hardwood floor, he stretched back on the couch with one arm across his eyes.

Yes, that had been the last night he had seen his sister. And the rest of his childhood had been spent listening to his parents fight, his mom crying in their room when she thought no one was listening, and fighting back his own tears when he had to spend all his time alone. He remembered wishing his dad would play with him, but it never happened again after that night. His dad suddenly had a lot more work at the office which turned into overnight trips no one ever bothered to explain to him. His mom wasn't much better. She still took care of him the way a mother should. He always had clean clothes and food on the table, but his house wasn't the same. She never hummed like she used to, never tickled him, never even asked him how his day had been at school. It was like when Meghan had left that night, his parents had left too, leaving behind two people who only looked like them. He started hating Meghan then. As bad as that night was, he would give anything if that had been the end of the story. But there was so much more.

Chapter Forty-One

November 2016

Kayleigh was nervous about meeting Meghan. She had tried to listen to music and even a podcast or two, but nothing seemed to work. Settling on silence for the rest of the drive, she tried not to think about all the things that could go wrong. Somehow not hearing anything at all was louder than when the radio had been blaring. Each minute felt like at least an hour until she finally pulled up in front of the coffee shop.

Wishing she had asked Meghan to describe what she looked like, Kayleigh got out of her car and walked toward the open door. The smell of fresh coffee wafted out toward her, but it did little to ease her discomfort. Finding the nearest table, she settled in, looking at her phone for a new text from the woman who was hopefully going to answer all her questions soon.

When her phone alerted her a few minutes later that she had a message, she was glad to see it was from Meghan, letting her know she had just pulled into the parking lot in a green jeep. Looking out the window in time to see a woman with blonde hair hopping down from the driver's seat, Kayleigh gasped. Nothing could have prepared her for what the woman looked like. Her hair was stringy, like it hadn't been washed recently, and her clothes hung on her like they were at least two sizes too big. Kayleigh forced a smile she didn't feel when the other woman walked toward her table.

Meghan couldn't believe it when she saw the woman sitting at the table It didn't take more than a glance to see what Robbie had seen in her. With her jet-black hair and blue eyes, she looked like she belonged on the cover of one of the magazines Meghan had always thought she would work for. She laughed a little as she thought about how the closest she ever got to a magazine article these days was when she was putting out stock at the grocery store where she worked. Life sure had mocked her.

Kayleigh stood up and reached out her hand toward Meghan, trying not to stare when the other woman's fingers touched her own. She had seen short nails before, but Meghan had apparently been biting hers for a long time. They weren't really there, just the tiniest reminder of where nails used to be. It physically hurt Kayleigh to look at them, so she looked away as she said, "Meghan? Have a seat. What would you like to drink? My treat."

"Black coffee is fine. Or water. I don't really care."

Feeling a bit guilty as she ordered herself a vanilla latte, Kayleigh placed the order for both of them before returning to the table. She suddenly felt the need to ease into her questions. The poor woman staring at her seemed ready to bolt any second. She couldn't help but wonder what would make someone look so sad. Hoping her husband wasn't the reason behind what she was seeing, she asked, "How was the drive? Mine was nerve-wracking, to tell you the truth."

Meghan couldn't help but like this woman even though she was very intimidated by her. She was just so perfect. Her clothes fit like they had been made for her, and she even had matching polish on her fingers and toes. She was everything a woman should be. Meghan thought about all the times she had sat at their vanity with Sarah when they were kids, looking in the mirror as they fixed each other's make-up. The woman who shared her table was what they had each hoped to look like one day. Meghan didn't need a mirror to tell her nothing could be further from the truth. She only hoped she didn't smell. She couldn't quite remember how many days it had been since she had taken a shower. It usually wasn't something that bothered her, but sitting across the table from the woman who had married Robbie made her all too aware of everything that was wrong with her. Turning her attention back to the woman and the question she had just asked her, she answered, "Um, sorry. Sometimes I get lost in thought. I mean, yes, the ride was okay, I guess. The jeep didn't break down, you know?"

Not knowing quite what to do with such an odd answer, Kayleigh decided to change the subject a bit as she said, "This must be weird for you, hearing from a stranger like this. I've been trying to put some pieces of my husband's past together and your name came up. Do you remember a lot about Robert?"

Choking on the sip of coffee she had just put in her mouth, Meghan cleared her throat before answering, "Yeah, I remember a lot about Robbie. He kind of ruined my life, so there's that. You don't forget guys like him." Taking another swallow to calm her nerves, she went on, "Look, I'm sorry. I'm guessing you loved him or you wouldn't be here, but it wasn't like that for me. I mean, I loved him, but I wasn't old enough. Or good enough. I don't really know. I just wasn't enough, okay?"

Pain tore through Kayleigh as she watched the other woman's face. When she talked, she looked like a little girl. Wondering for the first time if Meghan might be mentally unstable, she softly asked, "Did he hurt you?"

Meghan fought hard to keep the rage in her heart off her face. How was she supposed to answer that? Yeah, he ripped her heart out, ruined her life, stole her family from her, and killed her sister. Is that what this nice lady wanted to hear about her dead husband? Thinking not, she merely said, "Yeah, you could say that."

Finishing her drink, Kayleigh struggled to know whether to push for more. She wanted answers, but she also wanted to be kind. This woman looked ready to break down any minute. Smiling at her, she settled with the kindest words she could think of as she told her, "I'm sorry. I don't need to know what he did, but I want you to know I'm sorry. Is there anything I can do for you?"

"There's nothing anyone can do for me."

"Trent said something about your parents…"

Cutting her off quickly, Meghan said, "Look, I gotta go. I thought maybe I could help you, but this is just too much. I'm happy for whatever you and Robbie had and all, but that has nothing to do with me. My life ended a long time ago." Getting up to leave, she turned her back on Kayleigh and walked out of the coffee shop.

Sitting there with her mouth open a bit, Kayleigh watched her hop back into the jeep and drive away. She hadn't considered that she would be leaving this meeting with more questions than answers, but she was. Talk about dead ends.

Cleaning up their empty cups and napkins before she made her way to her car, Kayleigh decided to spend the long drive doing the one thing she needed to do more often. She planned to pray for Meghan the entire way home.

Chapter Forty-Two

Waking up refreshed, Kayleigh stayed in bed for a few extra minutes. She couldn't remember the last time she had dreamed about Robert. Not sure it was a good thing, she hopped up from her bed and went to the bathroom. After she securely fastened her robe around herself, she made her way to her new chaise lounge. Grabbing her Bible from the table she kept close by, she opened it to the book of Ruth. She had been reading the Bible every morning since she had met Meghan for coffee. She felt a strong urge to read about all the women in the Bible. She didn't know why, but it almost felt like she was storing up hope for the other woman or something. It didn't make sense to her, but she had learned long ago that when it came to God, she needed to just obey. She didn't need to rely on what she thought was normal. She was learning more and more every day how truly little she actually knew.

As she read, she thought about how much Ruth had lost. She wondered why there was so much sadness in life. Even as she pondered it all, she knew she would never understand. The more time that had passed since Robert's death, the more she realized that life didn't always play fair. More than that though, she was beginning to understand that there was more to living than just being happy. There was a difference between being happy and having joy which had become clearer to her every day. Spending time with the Lord in prayer had been a real eye-opener for her too. She couldn't deny this quiet time had made all the difference. She could now see how she had been trying to figure out everything on her own. The more time she spent praying, the more she had learned to let go. The more she read her Bible, the more she understood answers sometimes come more slowly than at other times. The only thing she was required to do was to wait patiently which was sounding like an easier thing to do every day, and she was so grateful.

This morning, as she studied about Ruth, she couldn't get Meghan out of her mind. The woman didn't have the strength and maybe not even the faith of Ruth, but she had suffered a loss. In fact, it was that loss that kept her on Kayleigh's mind.

She felt drawn to her somehow, and as she finished her morning time with Jesus, she made a decision. She knew it was time to call Meghan Jefferson again, time to reach out to her in kindness. She wouldn't demand answers. In fact, she didn't plan to ask a single question. She wanted to offer her the gift of friendship. She could only pray that Meghan would want to be her friend too.

*

Meghan just stared at the phone before reading the text message again. She couldn't understand why Robbie's widow wouldn't leave her alone. It wasn't like she had exactly been warm and fuzzy to the other woman when they had met at the coffee shop. Curiosity got the better of her, so she sent back a quick reply agreeing to meet up later in the week.

When the time came for them to meet again, she didn't have to wonder who she was looking for like last time. And somehow Kayleigh didn't seem as intimidating as she had the first time they met. Maybe it was the way she was wearing a pair of jeans and a soft blue sweatshirt, or maybe it was the kindness shining in her eyes. It didn't really matter to Meghan why she felt more comfortable, she was just glad she did.

When Kayleigh went to get drinks for them, this time she didn't bother asking Meghan what she wanted. She took a chance and ordered two lattes piled high with whipped cream for both of them. On a whim, she added a few muffins to their order. She figured what they didn't eat, Meghan could take home. The poor thing looked like she could blow away. Kayleigh knew some women liked to be on the skinny side, but this went way beyond that. She knew there was a lot more to Meghan's story. She surprised herself with her genuine concern, and also by how Robert hadn't crossed her mind one time since she had stepped foot in the coffee shop.

Chapter Forty-Three

"Becca, you look great. Why are you so worried?"

Unable to stop the blush as it quickly covered her cheeks, Becca wished her friend would stop smiling. Yes, she and Kevin were finally going out on a real date, but she was too old to feel this nervous. It didn't help that her best friend was treating her like a young girl with a crush. With a little more force than necessary, she tugged on the scarf in Kayleigh's hand before saying, "I do not look great. I need to lose at least thirty pounds and you know it."

"Hey, I was just messing with you. I'm sorry. You really are worried, aren't you?"

"Yes, I really am. Oh, I just like him so much. What if I'm reading more into this than he is? I don't think I can take it if he breaks my heart."

"Um, that's definitely not something you need to worry about. Have you looked around your house lately? Exactly how many vases of roses are in here anyway? A guy who's going to break your heart doesn't drop a ton of money on flowers before that kind of date. No, my friend, Kevin is thinking pretty much the same thing you are."

Smiling for the first time all night, Becca grabbed the scarf again, more gently this time. Tying it around her neck, she said, "I'm sorry. I know I'm being silly. Now tell me about what's been going on with Meghan."

"Becca, it's been amazing. We've had coffee together several times. She's actually starting to look better too, you know? But it's so much more than that. I like her. I like her a lot. You would too. I would love for the three of us to get together, but I don't think she's quite ready for that yet. Even though I haven't brought Robert up again, I can tell she wants me to. I think next time we meet, I'll ask her about him again. It's funny how everything has changed, you know? I still think Robert wanted me to know about his past, but I no longer feel that mad desire to learn about it. I think Meghan is going to have quite a story to tell me, and I'd be lying if I didn't say it's going to be hard to hear, but I think I'm ready. More importantly, I think she's ready to tell it.

Reaching out to hug her friend, Becca said, "You're really something else, you know that? I'm so proud of you, and Robert would be proud of you too. No matter what you find out from Meghan, you're going to be okay, aren't you?"

Kayleigh sighed before she answered, "Yeah, I really am."

Picking up her purse and car keys, Becca said a quick good-bye before she left her house. She had made plans to meet Kevin at the restaurant and didn't want to be late. She knew Kayleigh would lock the door behind her when she left. Somehow having a few minutes alone with her best friend made this night that held so much promise even better.

*

Kayleigh knew she was doing a much better job at work, but the promotion still surprised her. Her boss had been so gracious to her when Robert had died and in the months that followed, months when she couldn't seem to get her act together. Once she started feeling more like herself, she had made an effort to be an even better employee than she had been before the accident. Although money had never crossed her mind, she had to admit it was nice to see the increase in her paycheck.

Looking at the photo of her husband that still sat in the same spot on her desk, she thought about how proud he would be of her. She still missed him desperately, but since the dreams had stopped, she had finally been able to gain a little perspective. She knew she was moving forward at a healthy and steady pace. He would always be the love of her life, but she no longer felt that life wasn't worth living. She smiled as she pictured him giving her a high-five and one of his killer smiles. She had been blessed to be married to him for so long. She was grateful she could now focus on what they had together rather than all they had lost. It made all the difference.

Chapter Forty-Four

Trent had lost count of how many nights he had gotten drunk. He knew he had to get his act together soon. The money he had saved while working at the fire station was running out. He knew he needed to find another job soon, but he didn't know where to start.

All those months working with Robert Wilson had taught him a lot about himself. He had actually thought they were going to have a real relationship. It didn't matter to him that it was a little one-sided; he was getting enough from the older man to make him happy. If only he hadn't walked by Chief's office that night. If only he hadn't slowed down when he heard the anger in their voices. If only he hadn't learned that not only did his mentor know who he was, but that he saw him as a burden.

Hands fisted in a deep and sudden rage, Trent had walked away from the office door before he could hear the rest of their conversation. He knew what he had to do, and it couldn't happen fast enough for him.

*

May 2015

"What are you doing now?"

"I was just checking the hall. Didn't you hear footsteps? I don't want any of the other guys finding out about any of this."

"Was anyone out there?"

"Nah. Look, I'm sorry I got so mad. It's just that the kid has really been driving me nuts lately. I'll keep trying though. Even though he's a royal pain, he deserves a chance as much as the next guy. I just wish he wasn't Meghan's brother, you know? It gets to me every single time I see his face."

"I hear ya. You can't make all that go away, but maybe it's not an accident that he's here. Maybe this is how you can make it up to her. And to Sarah."

Running his hand over his lips like he did so often now, Robert said, "Yeah, maybe."

"Okay, get back to work. And go find the rookie, okay? You're stuck with him for the rest of the shift, so just make the best of it."

Robert left his friend's office and went in search of the young man who had been the topic of their heated conversation. He knew he needed to work on his attitude. No one deserved to be treated wrong, and he was determined to do whatever it took to make Trent feel at home. He certainly didn't think they would ever be friends, but that didn't mean he couldn't at least try to accept him as part of his station family. After all, you didn't exactly get to choose who was in your family.

Chapter Forty-Five

November 2016

Meghan was ready to share her story with her new friend. She couldn't believe she was actually thinking of Robbie's wife as a friend. Life sure had a funny way of surprising her. She wasn't sure what good could come from telling Kayleigh about her past, but she knew the other woman had to be curious even though she thankfully hadn't asked about it since their first meeting.

Unable to believe she was actually going to be the one to bring it up first, she made sure she got to the coffee shop early. Ordering their usual lattes and muffins, she was glad she had arrived in time to pay for their treat. She was starting to feel a bit like a charity case, and she knew that was no way to be a true friend. It still seemed impossible that someone like Kayleigh could actually want to spend time with someone like her, but the more time they spent together, the easier it was to believe.

Looking up when she heard the tiny bell ring, she smiled when she saw who had walked through the door. When Kayleigh reached down to give her a light hug, she was pleased not to flinch like she had the first few times it had happened. It had been so long since she had let anyone touch her, and it had taken some time to get used to accepting hugs again. Now she was surprised at how much she actually looked forward to being held. Her childhood had been cut short, and it had been so long since she had even felt her mother's touch. That had been one of the hardest things to deal with after Sarah had died, after she had moved in with their Aunt Linda. When she had finally moved back home, her parents never treated her the same way again. Her mother didn't seem to have a moment to spare for her, so she grew used to being alone. Over the years, it had become her preferred way to live. She had pushed everyone away who had even tried to get too close. The irony was not lost on her that the wife of the person who had caused every single one of her problems was the one who had finally broken through her shell.

*

Chief dreaded the phone call he was about to make. Having no desire to ever speak to Trent Jefferson again, he had literally groaned out loud when the paperwork had landed on his desk. He couldn't believe he had forgotten to get the kid to sign these forms. It wasn't like him to make such careless mistakes which was further proof of how much he was still reeling from Robbie's death. But he was the chief of this fire station, and he couldn't allow his personal feelings to interfere with his job.

"Yeah."

If he didn't know better, he would bet the kid was drunk. Glancing at the clock on his desk, he confirmed that it was indeed only ten in the morning. He wondered what time a person would have to start drinking to already be that drunk by ten o'clock. Deciding to give the other man the benefit of the doubt, he asked, "Did I wake you up?"

"Uh, no. Who is this anyway?"

"Yeah, sorry about that. This is Chief Preston. Is this Trent Jefferson?"

"Chief? I sure didn't expect to hear from you again. What do you need?"

"I actually need you to come down to the station soon. I forgot to have you sign a few papers. Nothing big, but it might help you out with insurance down the road."

"Today's not good, but I'll stop by in a few days, okay?"

Chief looked at the phone in his hand. The rookie had hung up on him. He'd be mad if it wasn't so funny. Who acted like that anyway? It must be because the kid was drunk. As much as he wanted to, he knew he wouldn't tease him about it when he came in. He didn't want to get too close to him. The sooner he put every part of his past behind him, the better.

Chapter Forty-Six

Becca was praying hard. She knew Kayleigh was excited about getting to know Meghan so well, but she couldn't help but have her suspicions. What if the other woman wasn't what she seemed to be? Kayleigh seemed to think she was helping Robert's old girlfriend, but Becca couldn't help but wonder if her friend was actually strong enough to be much good to anyone. It worried her to think she might be much more fragile still than she let on. Sure, things had seemed so much better since the dreams had stopped, but that didn't mean Kayleigh didn't still have her dark moments. Knowing prayer wasn't a last resort but the only way her friend would find peace, Becca stayed on her knees, talking to the One who loved her friend more than she did.

*

Meghan was getting nervous. She could tell Kayleigh was getting tired of the small talk, so she broached the subject she had been avoiding for several weeks. Talking as softly as she could, she said, "Kayleigh, I'm ready to tell you more about Robbie now. I appreciate you not asking again, but I can only imagine how you must be feeling right now. I've spent a lot of time thinking about it all, and the Robert you married isn't the same Robbie I knew as a kid. It actually took a lot of sleepless nights for me to figure that out if I'm being honest."

Sighing before responding, Kayleigh said, "Meghan, I gotta be honest with you. My mission at first was to get to the bottom of this whole thing. I knew he had a secret, but I didn't figure that out until after he died. And as desperate as I was to know what it was, I'm really not anymore. Sure, I'm still curious, but so much has changed for me. I've been praying for you a lot, and I've been reading my Bible more too. It started as a way to understand and help you, but it's actually helped me so much more than I could ever explain. Please tell me what you need to, but you need to know that I'm really okay if we just keep being friends."

"I definitely want to stay friends. You're the first person I've been comfortable talking to since my sister. Sarah was my best friend. I can't explain how much I miss her, but the guilt. Oh, Kayleigh, the guilt has eaten me alive for so long. It took a long time for me to put all the pieces together, and when I finally figured it out? Well, it just about did me in."

"What was it about Sarah that made you feel so guilty?"

"This is going to be hard for you to hear, but I have to tell you the whole story in order for you to understand. I'm assuming you know some of this, but I'm just going to start at the beginning anyway. Is that okay?"

Reaching over to pat her hand, Kayleigh told her, "Whatever you need to say is good with me, but you really don't have to tell me any of it."

"I know, and I appreciate that, but I really want to. Sarah was so young when she met Robbie. It was one of the first days of school when he started paying attention to her, and she couldn't have been more thrilled. It was no more than two weeks before he had asked for her phone number. Man, I've never seen her so happy. She had a serious crush on him from the minute she laid eyes on him. Who could blame her? I mean, he was seriously hot. Sorry, I know you guys were married, but he was."

Laughing a little, Kayleigh agreed, "You should have seen him in his bunker gear. My heart definitely skipped a beat every time I saw him too."

"Yeah, well, it's still weird to talk about this with you, you know? But anyway, Sarah dated him for a few months. One night I went to one of his basketball games with her. I was only in the eighth grade, just a baby really, but you couldn't tell me anything. I looked at Robbie in his uniform that night and something shifted. I could see in his eyes that he had felt it too. It wasn't a week before he dumped Sarah and took me out on my first date ever. I had to keep it a secret though. I mean, she was my sister, and we really were best friends."

"She sounds perfect."

"She was. We had big plans too. We had basically mapped out our entire life and we were going to live it together, but then I made some terrible decisions. Dating a senior was my first wrong choice. I didn't know a thing about guys, but I knew

I wanted to keep him for myself, so I let him believe I had done more than I had. I know you don't want to hear this part, so I'll skip right to what you need to know. I got pregnant, but I never got the chance to tell him. He dumped me the night I rode my bike to his house to break the news. I told Sarah, and she confronted him about it later. I overheard him and Mark talking about it before her funeral. They didn't know I was there. Robbie was pretty messed up about it, and it sounded like Sarah had really freaked out in front of him. She died because of me. She died because she was so upset about me and Robbie and the baby."

"And you've been carrying this pain around for so long. Meghan, I'm so sorry, but even if she was upset, you know it wasn't your fault she died, right? I mean, it was just an accident."

"There's more, but I just can't. I didn't know talking about it would be like this. I'm physically exhausted right now. I've never told that story to anyone, ever, and I didn't know it would be so hard. I think I need to go home now and lie down. Can I finish telling it to you later?"

"Of course. I meant what I said earlier. You really don't have to tell me all of this unless you want to. Please know I'll be praying for you."

Standing up to leave, Meghan reached out and gave her a hug before walking out of the coffee shop without saying another word. She had a feeling the next conversation they had might not end with her receiving a hug and a promise of prayer.

Chapter Forty-Seven

"Becca, she was so upset. And she said there was more. I couldn't exactly tell her I already knew about the abortion, but I feel so bad that she thinks I don't know. That's not exactly the type of thing you casually drop into a conversation, but how do I let her know she doesn't need to tell me? I mean, without telling her I already know. I just hate that she has to even think about what she did, much less talk about it."

"Kayleigh, you're okay, right? I can tell you're feeling much happier lately, but are you still looking for the missing piece of the puzzle?"

"I'd be lying if I told you I'm not still curious, but if you go into the den, you'll have your answer. Just look on my puzzle table. There's a brand new puzzle dumped out with only the edges put together, but I'm excited about working on it."

"So, no more Robert Project? You've put away all the dream descriptions?"

"For now. I mean, I might pull them out again one day, but

it's no longer keeping me up at night. I think I'm okay if I never learn the whole story though. I think meeting Meghan and seeing the pain she's in has been the key for me. It's like getting to know her has made me realize just how incredibly young they both were when all this went down."

"I get it. As long as you're okay, that's all that matters. So, when are you going to see her again?"

"Not until this weekend. It really wiped her out to talk about it. I could see it on her face. I'm sure she went home and took the world's longest nap. We've texted a few times, but neither one of us has brought up Robert again. I don't have the heart to, and I honestly don't think she has enough energy to think about him right now."

*

Trent was not looking forward to stepping foot inside the fire station again. He couldn't wrap his head around looking any of the other men in the eyes, especially Chief. He couldn't stop feeling like they would all see right through him, straight through to the person he really was. But he knew he had to tie up loose ends if he was going to put this all behind him, so he made his way to Chief's office at the back of the station.

"Trent, good to see you."

When the older man didn't get up out of his chair or extend his hand, Trent knew something was up. He was used to the chief always being friendly, but it sure seemed like he was getting the cold shoulder for some reason. Wanting to appear as casual as possible, he said, "So, where do I sign?"

"Have a seat. There are quite a few papers you need to look at before you sign them."

Sitting down, Trent accepted the clipboard and pen his old boss offered him. After he had signed the last paper, he stood up to leave before asking, "That all?"

"Yeah, but before you leave can I ask you a question?"

"About?"

"About the night Robert Wilson died."

"We've been over that enough. Man, I've told you all I know." Standing up and walking toward the door, he turned around before adding, "Just let it go, okay?"

Watching the young man's back as he stormed out of the fire station did little to ease Chief's mind. If he had his suspicions before, his senses were now on high alert. The kid definitely knew more than he was telling. Wondering if opening the investigation up again would cause everyone more pain, Kayleigh's face came to his mind. As far as he could tell, she was just now moving on from Robbie's death. Thinking about her was all the answer he needed. Did he think Trent Jefferson was hiding something? Absolutely. Would he drag it all up again and risk causing Kayleigh to relive all that pain she had finally started letting go? There was no way. Whatever the rookie fire fighter knew just walked out of the fire station with him. Chief hated it, but he knew he wouldn't chase the kid down for answers. Sometimes having peace was more important than knowing the truth. He could only hope he'd never have to explain that to his best friend's widow.

Chapter Forty-Eight

When Kayleigh walked into the coffee shop, the first thing she noticed was how much better Meghan looked. She looked refreshed in a way she hadn't before. And eager. The woman had this look about her that Kayleigh couldn't quite explain. Wanting to skip the small talk, she went to the table and asked, "Do you still want to tell me the rest of the story?"

Meghan was glad she had slipped a bottle of water into her purse. She knew they wouldn't be ordering coffee until after they talked. She hoped Kayleigh would stick around that long, but her friend was waiting for an answer, so she said, "Yeah. I'm ready."

Sitting down in the chair opposite her, Kayleigh asked, "Would it be okay if I prayed for us first? I have the strongest urge to ask God to be here at this table with us."

Touched by the offer, Meghan could only whisper, "Yes."

After she prayed, Kayleigh felt a burden lift off her. She had wanted to pray because she suspected reliving the abortion would be incredibly painful. It didn't make sense the way the prayer felt like it was more for her than for Meghan though. She smiled a little as she thought about how God never made any mistakes. It pleased her to know He cared about her as much as He did Meghan. Sure, it was hard knowing her husband had been with someone else, and it was devastating to think his child had died, but it was something she had honestly thought she had come to terms with. Judging by the way the prayer had affected her, she must not have been doing as well as she thought. But right now her focus needed to be on Meghan, so she said, "I'll just listen. Don't worry about me interrupting or anything. I'm here for you, okay?"

Believing every word she had just heard, Meghan jumped in where she had left the story at their last visit, "This next part is a lot harder to share. You see, I told Sarah about the baby, but I was so messed up, I just couldn't share the rest with her."

When Meghan paused, it took everything in Kayleigh to stay true to her promise. She wanted to blurt out that she already knew about the abortion. She desperately wanted to stop her from having to talk about it, but she felt the strongest urge to say nothing at all, so she waited silently for the other woman to go on.

"I've wondered so many times how my life would have been different if I had told Sarah everything. I was too young to really understand it all, so I didn't pick up on what my sister was thinking. It wasn't until I overheard Robbie and Mark talking at the funeral home. One of them used the word abortion and then started talking about Sarah. I was furious. All I could think was that he had gotten my sister pregnant too and then had taken her to a clinic. But then Mark said something that stopped me in my tracks. I almost couldn't get through my own sister's funeral after hearing it. All I could think about was what I had heard them say. I honestly don't think I heard one word our preacher said that day. You see, Mark was talking about me. They thought I had gotten an abortion. They said Sarah thought I had gotten an abortion. That must have devastated her. I know I was on her mind when she was driving her car that night. I'll never know if it was really an accident or not, but she died because of me. If she hadn't been upset because of an abortion I never had, then she wouldn't have ended up in the other lane."

Kayleigh knew now why God had made it so clear that she was just supposed to listen. She could barely hear her own voice when she asked, "But you were pregnant, right? If you didn't have an abortion, where's the baby?"

Meghan had tears in her eyes when she looked up and answered, "Oh yes, there was a baby. I moved away for a long time. I had him while I was gone, and then I brought him home to my parents. Everyone just thought my mom had gotten pregnant after Sarah died. She stayed inside the house for so many months in mourning that no one would have questioned not seeing her belly grow. No one ever suspected a thing. At least not that I ever knew about. I didn't stay there long before I moved back in with my Aunt Linda. I just couldn't handle being in the same house with the baby. My dad couldn't either, but at least he handled it better than I did. My mom though. Wow, my mom was a saint. She raised Trent as her own child, but I never could get in on the act. It hurt him so much to have a sister who didn't love him, but how could I? He was the reason my sister died."

"Trent? Wait, Trent's not your brother?" When the shock turned to realization, Kayleigh's hand flew up to her mouth as she whispered, "Trent Jefferson is Robert's son?"

"I'm so sorry. I can't imagine how they ended up working together. I promise Trent still thinks I'm his sister. He hates me. Hates our parents too. Everything got turned upside down when he was around ten. He became what the teachers called a problem child. If there was trouble to be found, he stepped right into it. He had been so good until then too. My mistake with Robbie ruined more than just my life."

"Look, I'm really glad you told me this, but I need some time to process it all. Do you mind if we skip our lattes today?"

Hoping she didn't look as disappointed as she felt, Meghan readily agreed to cutting their visit short. She couldn't help but wonder if this would be the last time she saw her new friend. She knew she had laid a lot on her, and as much as she liked the other woman, she wouldn't blame her if she never wanted

to see her again.

Chapter Forty-Nine

"Slow down, I can't understand a word you're saying when you talk that fast." Becca was worried about her friend. She could kick herself too. Wasn't this exactly what she had been afraid would happen if Kayleigh got too close to Meghan?

"Sorry. It's just a lot. Okay, like I was saying, Meghan never got an abortion. I don't know what that means. I mean, I know what it means, but I don't know what Robert knew. She told me that Trent is Robert's child. Becca, do you think he kept his son a secret from me all these years?"

"Whoa! Okay, let's think about it for a minute. If he had known his son all these years, that would mean he knew who Trent was. I just don't think that's true."

"Becca! I just thought of something. Chief and Robert were so close. Do you think Chief was lying to me when he told me about that essay and the way he figured out that Trent was Meghan's brother?"

"Why would he do that? He had already told you so much

that Robert had wanted to keep from you. It makes no sense that he would create a story like that. Why mention Trent at all, you know?"

"Yeah, I guess. I think I'm going to head to the station to see him though. If he lied to me, that's one thing, but if Trent being Robert's son is something even Chief didn't know, then maybe he can help me make some sense of it all."

"Want me to go with you? I can be dressed and out of here in ten minutes."

"No, I'm good. I'm already in my car. I just can't wait another second."

"Okay, but let me know what he says. Seriously. Don't try to deal with this on your own. Promise?"

"Promise. Thanks again."

"You know it. Bye."

"Bye."

*

Chief saw Kayleigh's car as soon as she pulled into the station parking lot. He wasn't expecting her today and judging by the way she slammed her car door, she wasn't here to deliver cookies. Something had definitely upset her, and he could only hope he would have answers to whatever questions she would be throwing at him soon.

He had almost made it to his office door when it swung open, revealing the flushed face of his friend's widow. Not waiting for an invitation, she sat down and immediately started to cry.

"Kayleigh, what in the world is wrong?" Thinking a hug might not be his best move at this point, he made his way around his desk, sat down, and moved a pile of files aside so he could look at her better.

Wiping her eyes with the sleeve of her sweatshirt, Kaleigh said, "I found something out that has totally changed all of this, everything I thought I knew. I don't know if you already knew, but I want to ask one thing of you. Please just be honest with me, okay?"

Hoping he could tell her what she wanted, but still completely confused by what she was about to tell him, he answered, "Of course."

"There's no easy way to tell you this, but Trent Jefferson is not Meghan's brother." Seeing the shocked look on her husband's oldest friend's face gave her a small degree of comfort. At least he hadn't been lying to her. If only she could be as sure about her husband. She continued by softly adding, "Trent is Robert and Meghan's son."

"That's not possible. Meghan never had that baby."

"How do you know that? How did you and Robert ever really know that?"

"That's what Sarah was so upset about the night she died. Robbie just couldn't deal with it though. To be honest, I've never thought about it before now, but you're right. He never confronted Meghan about it. But if she was pregnant, wouldn't we have known? Wouldn't she have begun to show?"

"Not if she moved away. She did, you know. I've actually become pretty close to her, and she's shared a lot with me. Not everything, but enough."

"I can't believe this."

"Here's something else to think about. Do you really think it was a coincidence that Trent applied for a job at the same station as his father? Do you think he told Robert? How much do you think Robert knew?"

"Kayleigh, Robbie was my best friend. I think I knew him pretty well. He died thinking his only baby had died because of an abortion. He thought Trent was Meghan's brother. We talked about it a few times, so I know it's true. Look, he didn't even want to work with the kid at first because he frankly never wanted to think about that part of his past again. I'm confused though. Trent never once let on that he knew who Robbie was."

"I'm going to call him."

"I don't think that's such a good idea. He wasn't in a good place the last time I saw him. And I think he was drunk when we talked on the phone. Why don't you let me reach out to him? I got him in here once to sign some papers. I think I can make up something to get him to come back, and once he's in this office I promise I'll get to the bottom of all this."

Standing up, Kayleigh wrapped her arms around herself as she agreed, "Please do it soon. I can't stand not knowing."

"I'll call him as soon as you leave, and I'll do my best to get him to come in right away."

"I'll keep my phone on me. Please call?"

Walking her to the door, he squeezed her shoulder as he said, "Of course."

Long after she was gone, he stared at the phone on his desk. He knew what he had to do, but he dreaded it. He wasn't sure how he would react if he found out Robbie had lied to him for over two decades. He couldn't wrap his head around how that could even be possible.

Looking through the pile on his desk, he found Trent's file from the other day. Quickly thinking of an excuse to get the other man to come back to the station, he picked up the phone. No matter how much the truth might end up hurting him, he knew he had no choice but to place this call.

Chapter Fifty

Meghan had stayed up half the night thinking about her life. Everything had seemed so easy before she met Robbie. It had always been that way for her, she thought of her life as time before Robbie versus time after him. Her mistake with him had just been such a pivotal point in her life. If she could go back in time, she would, but she had stopped playing the what-if games years ago. Meeting Kayleigh had changed everything though. She was finally starting to see that the young boy she had thought she was in love with so long ago really was just that. He hadn't been that much older than she was. At the time, he had seemed more like a man than a boy, but meeting Kayleigh and hearing about their marriage had helped her understand how much he really had grown up. It even hurt her to think about all the pain he had carried with him all those years. For so long, she had felt like a martyr for keeping her pregnancy and their son from him. Somehow it had made her feel important to think she had made such a sacrifice. Now it sickened her to think how she had been the one to ruin so many lives. It pained her to think about how things could have been. If only she had been brave enough to tell Robbie the truth.

Knowing she couldn't call him and apologize like she wanted to, she thought about all the people she did need to reach out to. She couldn't let herself think about calling Trent, wasn't sure she would ever be that strong, but she could call her parents. First, she needed to talk to Kayleigh again. The woman had to be in so much pain right now. She would do whatever she could to take some of it away. Maybe, in that small way, she could finally make something good come out of all the bad that had been present most of her life.

*

Kayleigh had checked her phone at least a dozen times since leaving the station. If Chief didn't text her soon, she was seriously thinking about driving back over there. She trusted him, but what if he had gotten distracted? What if he had changed his mind about calling Trent and had just forgotten to let her know?

Deciding to go outside for a walk, she slipped her cell phone into the pocket of her jeans. She had to do something; waiting had never exactly been one of her strengths. Maybe a walk would help her focus on something other than what her Robert Project had turned into. She never could have predicted after that first dream that her search for the truth would bring her to her husband's child, a child she had never known even existed. Knowing her thoughts were going to take her to a bad place if she wasn't careful, Kayleigh looked around, trying to find some spot of beauty to distract her. The first thing to catch her eye was a small child kicking a ball in his front yard with his dad. Turning around abruptly, she decided to go back home. This walk had been a bad idea. She knew she needed to be patient, but just because she couldn't call Chief didn't mean she didn't have anyone to reach out to.

Pecking away at her phone a few minutes later, she sent a quick text to Meghan. As she waited for the reply she hoped would come, she went into her house to get ready. She had to believe that Meghan would agree to meet her for coffee. She had to talk to someone, and she hoped this woman who had become an unlikely friend would feel the same way.

*

Glad to read the text, Meghan was already walking to her jeep as she sent back a reply. She had been thinking about calling her all day, but she wasn't sure what she could say to make Kayleigh feel better. She was tired of sitting around and worrying though. Maybe if she talked to her new friend, she would finally find the strength to make that phone call to her parents. She didn't dare think about calling Trent yet, but she knew she could dream that he would accept her apology someday.

When they both pulled into the parking lot at the same time, Meghan had to smile. They had come such a long way since the first time they had met each other here. She hoped this visit wouldn't be awkward. She hoped she could somehow comfort Kayleigh today.

"Hey, thanks for meeting me. I've got a lot to tell you."

"Let's grab our drinks and muffins and go find a quiet table. I'm really glad you sent that text. I literally was about to send you one and suggest the same thing."

Hugging Meghan as they walked to the counter to place their orders, Kayleigh silently said a prayer. She wanted to do the right thing, but she also didn't want to cause this sweet woman more pain. It still devastated her to know Robert had been part of the problem, but she knew he would be proud of her for trying to help everyone find closure. As much as she wanted to feel better, somewhere along the way her focus had shifted. She now wanted to help everyone who had been hurt by the person her husband once was. She knew he would do it himself if he were still here.

Once they were seated and sipping their lattes, Meghan said, "I've been thinking about calling my parents. I'm definitely not ready to reach out to Trent yet, and I'm sure he isn't ready to hear from me, but I think it's time to call my mom and dad. Past time. I was so upset at them for so long, but lately I've been thinking about it all. Really thinking. Mom basically laid down her own life when Trent was born. I can see now that she did it all for me. I was a selfish girl back then. I know my dad was mad most of the time, but I can appreciate now that he was more hurt than anything else. I was too young to be a mother, but I was also too young to have done what made me a mother. No wonder he couldn't stand to look at me."

"You were just a kid. I wish I could make it better for you, but I know as well as anyone else that we can't change our past. I do have a question though. Did your parents really think they could keep you a secret from Trent? Did they intend for him to never find out that you were his mother?"

"I don't know. To be honest, I still don't think of myself that way. It's hard to explain, but I avoided him as much as possible from the moment he was born. My mom used to beg me to pay him some attention. I remember when he would cry at night, I would put my hands over my ears or listen to music just so I wouldn't have to hear his little voice. I never once changed his diaper or fed him a bottle, and I rarely played with him. I finally moved out again just to get away from him, and he was just an innocent baby. My mom must have been so exhausted. When I came back years later for a rare visit, we had an epic fight. I think Trent heard too much that night because he never looked at me the same way again. And he completely stopped trying to get my attention too. Long story short, he absolutely hates me now."

"Do you think he ever suspected anything?"

Meghan's laugh came out sounding a bit more like a cry when she said, "Oh, he probably does. I'm guessing that's why he won't go near Mom and Dad now. I have no idea how much he's figured out though. You know, they gave up their life for us and this is how we repay them? They have a daughter who had to die because of their other daughter's mistake and their only grandchild hates them. All because of me."

"I don't know what to say. I'm sorry. You don't know how much I wish Robert was sitting here with us right now. He always acted like he wanted to tell me something, but he never seemed able to get it out. I was too wrapped up in myself to really pay much attention to my own husband sometimes. I think we both have stuff to feel guilty about."

"Well, I think I win if this is a contest."

"I'm sorry. I wasn't trying to compare my life with yours. Really."

"No, it's good. I'm just on edge. Digging all of this up again has been good in some ways, but it also has been very painful for me."

"You know I'm here for you if you ever need me, right?"

"I do."

When her phone chimed a few seconds later, Kayleigh looked at Meghan. When her friend gave her a supportive nod, she looked at the screen and read the message from Chief.

"It's from Chief. He said Trent is on his way to the station. We should know something soon."

"Look, I'm a bundle of nerves, and I think I need to go home. I think maybe the long drive will help calm me down. Do you mind if I just wait to hear from you after you find out what Trent had to say? I just don't think I can deal with the play-by-play."

Not really understanding, Kayleigh pretended like she did when she said, "Of course. I promise to be in touch. Soon."

Within minutes, they had the table cleared and were both in their vehicles heading in different directions. Looking in the rearview mirror, Kayleigh didn't miss the way Meghan wiped her tears off her face. As hard as being childless had been for her, she knew the pain Meghan was feeling had to be much worse. She couldn't imagine the agony of giving up a child and watching him grow up without being able to tell him who you were. It must have been awful. Praying for her like she did so often now, Kayleigh asked the Lord to let Meghan feel His love. She asked Him to also help the entire Jefferson family find peace. If anyone deserved it, their family certainly did.

Chapter Fifty-One

Trent knew he needed to get out of his car, but thoughts of Robert Wilson wouldn't leave his head. Hitting the steering wheel with the palms of his hands, he reminded himself to get his act together. He had one more form to sign, then he would be finished with all of this.

When he entered the fire station, he was surprised to see Chief standing at the door waiting for him. The man was usually holed up in his office, so Trent immediately knew this was important.

"Trent, come on into the kitchen. I was just about to fix a cup of coffee. Can I get you something too?"

"Yeah, I guess coffee sounds good."

Grabbing two mugs from the cabinet, Chief quickly filled them with the dark brew he was so fond of. Offering one to Trent, he sipped his own while watching the other man look around for the sugar bowl.

"Sorry, I forgot you don't take yours black. Take your time

and fix it like you want it. I'll be waiting in my office, okay?"

"Sure."

Pulling a spoon out of the drawer, Trent scooped sugar out of the bowl three times, taking his time to carefully tap it into his mug. Opening the refrigerator, he grabbed the half gallon of skim milk and added a generous splash before stirring it until the once-black liquid turned the nice light brown shade he loved so much. Finally, he put his dirty spoon in the sink. Knowing he couldn't stall any longer, he made his way back to his old boss's office. It was now very obvious to him that the other man had called him in to do more than just sign one form.

"Have a seat. There's no form for you to sign, but I'm guessing you already figured that out. I really called you in because we need to talk."

Instantly feeling wetness under his arms, Trent tried to sound casual as he asked, "About what?"

"Robert Wilson."

"Okay. What could I possibly help you with?"

Not surprised at the sudden defensiveness in the kid's voice, Chief forced his own to stay calm as he said, "When you first applied, I figured out that you were related to Meghan. I assumed you were her brother. Knowing their history, I told Robbie. I wanted the two of you to work together because I thought that by helping you he could make amends somehow. Now I find out you aren't Meghan's brother at all."

"Yeah?"

Relieved and disappointed at the same time, Chief wasn't surprised that Trent already knew what he was about to tell him. He asked, "So you knew who Robbie was the whole time? And you still came to work here?"

"I know it's messed up, but I thought if I could just be near him that, I don't know, that maybe we could be friends or something. But it didn't quite work out that way, did it?"

"What do you mean?"

Trent sighed heavily as he went on, "Look, it's no secret that the man thought I was a pest. Nothing I ever did was good enough for him. It was like living my childhood all over again."

"I gotta ask you one thing. Did you ever tell him who you were?"

"Not really."

"That's not an answer. Look, you either did or you didn't."

"I wanted to. That night in the fire. I saw him come into that room, and something just came over me. When I reached out to him, I sort of fell onto him or something. I wanted to let him know who I was, but he got all violent with me. It was like he hated me or something. I lost it. I mean, I guess what I mean is, all those years just opened up for me. I never knew I had so much rage in me until that night. And then he fell out that window, and I had lost my chance to tell him anything."

Chief had years of experience and knew exactly how to mask his feelings, but he was struggling right now. This man as good as admitted to killing his best friend, and all he could say was that he had lost the chance to say something. All he could imagine was that the younger man had suffered some sort of breakdown. Going through his options quickly, he decided the best thing he could do was to play along, so he said, "I'm sure you did your best. And I think Robbie would be proud of you."

When Trent's eyes lit up, Chief knew he had his answer. The young man had been hurt deeply, but that didn't mean he didn't need to be held responsible for what he had caused that night. Standing up, he knew the other man would recognize that as his cue to leave.

When Trent walked slowly back to his car a few minutes later, Chief reached for the phone on his desk. His first call was to the police; his second one was to Kayleigh. He couldn't believe he was about to break her heart all over again.

Chapter Fifty-Two

Kayleigh had looked at the little slips of paper so much her vision was starting to blur. Running her hand over the table, she watched as they all floated to the floor. Lacking the strength to pick them up, she went into the kitchen for a bottle of water. The picture of her and Robert stopped her in her tracks. How had she not seen it before? Her husband had been so young when that photo had been taken, and the resemblance between him and Trent was now so obvious to her. It was subtle, and she was sure most people wouldn't see it, but she did. It made her sad to think about all her husband had lost.

When her phone rang, she knew it was Chief. She had been waiting for his call. Dreading it if she were being honest. But she had started all of this and she knew she had to follow it through, so she answered with a near-silent, "Hello?"

"Kayleigh? It's Mark."

He hadn't called himself that in many years. Hearing it now

took her back to their time in college together, to when he had been the best man at their wedding, and to all the times they had hung out before he had become her husband's boss.

"Is something wrong?"

"I need you to come to the station, okay? It's official business about Robbie's accident."

Feeling her knees go weak, she said, "I don't understand."

"Look, I can't really explain this over the phone. Just head on over, okay? And be safe. Don't speed."

Not hearing a bit of humor in his voice scared her, so she agreed quickly before hanging up the phone. She couldn't help the feeling of dread that was causing her stomach to burn a little. She had expected him to call with news about Trent. It couldn't be a coincidence that after meeting with the rookie fire fighter he wanted her to come in. Resisting the urge to overthink like she often did, she took several deep breaths before grabbing her purse and car keys and heading out the door. She would be strong, no matter what she was told. She would make Robert proud.

Frozen in Time

*

Trent threw the empty beer can and laughed when it landed in front of the trash can where the other cans were. When Gracie cocked her head at him, he reached down to rub her ears. She was a good dog who deserved more than he could give her. He had been drinking steadily since he had gotten home from his meeting with the chief. He knew he had said too much, and he had been surprised when he was allowed to just walk out of the station. Maybe the older man hadn't understood what he had been trying to confess. Wouldn't that be just his luck? To finally own up to something he did only to have it misunderstood. His dad had been right. He really couldn't do anything right. He laughed as he thought about how both his dads had thought that. Sure, Robert Wilson had never said those words to him, but looks could say a lot. And the other man had definitely let him know what a disappointment he was. He hadn't missed the way he had looked at the other guys when he saw that Trent would be going out on the call with him that night. He had tried to not let it bother him, but that familiar rage had grabbed onto him, refusing to let go. He was so tired of feeling angry all the time. Maybe that's why he had told Chief what he had done, but he couldn't even confess to killing someone without messing it up. He opened another beer as he thought about what a loser he was.

*

Meghan didn't want to talk to anyone, but she didn't have the heart to just ignore the ringing of her phone. It had to be Kayleigh, and even though she wasn't ready to deal with whatever she was going to hear, she picked up her phone and looked at the screen.

Seeing Trent's number staring back at her almost caused her to drop it. Why would he be calling her? She had put his number in her phone on a whim even though she knew she wasn't ready to call him yet. Pushing the button that would start the conversation she was dreading, she said, "Hello?"

"Meghan? Yeah, it's Trent."

Listening to the way his voice slurred, she felt a sudden pain that made her grab her chest. He was drunk, and she was the person he had chosen to call. She wasn't sure how that should make her feel, but she thought it had to mean something. She hoped he was calling her because he wanted to make a connection, but something told her it wasn't going to be that kind of phone call.

"Trent, are you doing okay?"

Not missing the mirth in his voice, she listened as he said, "Yeah, just peachy. I had a really fun talk with my ex-boss. The police should be knocking on my door any minute now, but in usual Trent-like fashion, I couldn't even tell on myself right."

"What do you mean about telling on yourself? What would you have to tell on yourself about? Trent, are you sure you're okay? You aren't really making sense."

"Meghan, can we just cut to the chase? I spent the first ten years of my life thinking my own sister hated me. I just never could understand why. Then that night happened. You remember the night. Man, you guys sure did have an epic fight, and I heard way too much. It didn't take long for me to figure out the whole story. But you know what? I wasn't old enough to really understand what it all meant. It took me a few years, but I finally figured it all out. Meghan, how could you? How could Mom and Dad do this to me? I'm an orphan. Do you know how that feels?"

Meghan never thought this day would come, and now that it had she didn't know how to deal with it. This man on the other end of the phone sounded like the small child she remembered from so long ago. She could clearly hear the pain in his voice, and it broke her heart to know she was the one who put it there. She said the only words she knew to say, "I'm so sorry."

"Sorry? You can keep your sorry. You know what, I shouldn't have called you. It was so easy to give me away, wasn't it? Did you ever love me? Did he?"

"Trent, I can tell you've been drinking. Now's not really the time to talk about all this. Can I call you tomorrow?"

When he hung up, she wasn't all that surprised. For the first time in her life, she thought about how selfish she had been. She had always focused on her pain, on what Robbie had done to her, and now all she could see was how awful she was. She dropped her head into her hands as the tears came. She was finally crying for the right reason, for her son, and these tears felt like they might possibly someday lead her to a happy ending.

Chapter Fifty-Three

Kayleigh ended her call with Meghan and immediately sent Becca a text. Even though she knew the other woman had been busy with her new boyfriend, this was definitely best friend news. When her phone rang a few seconds later, she wasn't surprised.

"Hey."

"Hello yourself! What's going on? Is everything okay?"

"Can you come over just to talk?"

"Of course. Kayleigh, is it about your Robert Project?"

"Yeah, it is."

"I'll be right there."

"I'll go preheat the oven. The cookies will be ready by the time you get here."

Grateful for a friend who would drop everything for her, she hopped off the couch and went into the kitchen to whip up a batch of her semi-famous chocolate chip cookies. She had made them so many times she didn't even need the recipe.

When her doorbell rang about twenty minutes later, she knew she would need five more minutes to fulfill her promise of sugary goodness to her friend. Opening the door and giving Becca a hug before she had a chance to get all the way inside, she couldn't help the tears that instantly came to her eyes.

"Kayleigh, tell me everything."

Pulling her into the kitchen so she wouldn't burn the cookies, she sat down at the table hoping Becca would do the same. When she did, she said, "It's so much. I can't quite figure it all out. Do you really think Robert didn't know Trent was his son?"

"I don't know, but everything you've told me makes me believe Chief. I honestly think Robert thought Trent was Meghan's brother."

"But how did he keep all that from me? Why?"

Reaching out to hold her, Becca let Kayleigh cry. She let go long enough to turn off the oven before returning to hold her some more. Sometimes words weren't needed, and she knew just being with her friend was the only way to truly comfort her right now, so she stayed still until Kayleigh's tears slowly stopped falling. She listened silently as her friend shared with her the most recent visit with Chief and the way the investigation had been opened back up. It didn't surprise her; she had suspected foul play all along. She knew there was a lot her friend wasn't telling her, but she didn't want to pry. Something told her the truth would come out soon enough.

*

Long after Becca had left, Kayleigh sat at the kitchen table holding the picture of her and Robert from the refrigerator. She wished more than anything that he could be with her right now instead of a picture of him. She needed to help him get through all of this. She knew that wasn't even a rational thought, but her heart broke for her husband. She wished they had known the truth about Trent from the beginning, not only for Robert's sake but for his son's as well. It felt so weird to use her husband's name and the word son in the same sentence.

Putting the picture back under the magnet as she walked through the kitchen, she turned off all the lights as she made her way up to her bedroom. Her heart felt heavy. She knew there was more going on than what Chief had shared with her, but she couldn't let herself think about any of it right now. All she wanted to do was to fall into her bed and go to sleep. For the first night in a long time, she didn't wash her face or brush her teeth before she climbed under the covers. She fell asleep almost immediately, almost as soon as her head hit the pillow.

When she woke up, she wasn't sure what time it was. Looking around the room, she realized it had to be close to morning. She wouldn't need her alarm though. After the dream she had just had, she knew sleep was nowhere to be found.

In it, she had been in the fire with her husband. As horrible as it was to relive Robert's final moments, she somehow woke up thinking about Trent. It made no sense to her even though she had known the young man had been on the scene the night of the accident. In her dream, she had been Trent, and she had felt everything he was feeling. She now knew how pitiful he was, how he had felt so abandoned by everyone in his life. She couldn't help but want to reach out to him, but she knew Chief hadn't told her everything about his most recent meeting with the young man. Hoping to learn something that would help her understand Trent better, she decided to take a shower before sending the text that she knew might change her life. She could only hope Chief would tell her everything he knew.

Chapter Fifty-Four

Becca had a Bible verse running through her head, one that she just had to share with her best friend. Since that night at her house, she had prayed for Kayleigh like she never had before, and every time she did, Romans 8:28 came to her mind. She had always known its truth, had always known that God really did bring everything together for a reason. Nothing bad happened without Him knowing, and He could bring good from bad. She wasn't sure if she had the right words to help Kayleigh understand though.

*

Chief was glad to see Kayleigh again, but he had to admit he was getting tired of having so much drama in his life. He was ready for things to settle back down the way he liked them to be, but he also knew he had to tell her everything he now knew about the night her husband had died.

"Chief, thanks for talking to me about this. I have to tell you something first if that's okay?" When he nodded his head encouragingly at her, she added, "I had another dream. It was the night of the accident. I was Trent in the dream this time, but I don't really know what he was doing. I do know exactly how he felt though. I never knew that a person could feel so sad, so unwanted, so desperate. It was terrible. I know this is going to sound weird, but I almost want to adopt him on Robert's behalf now."

Knowing what she had just shared with him wasn't going to match the news he had to share, Chief gently said, "You're a good person, you know that? It's no wonder Robbie fell madly in love with you. But Kayleigh, here's the thing, when Trent came to see me the other day he told me some stuff. That's the real reason I opened the investigation back up after talking to the police." Slowing down to give her a minute to digest what he had told her so far, he softly added, "I hope you understand that I couldn't tell you this until it was official, but Trent confessed to causing Robbie's death."

"What? I don't understand. How is that even possible? Robert fell out a window."

"He didn't fall. He was pushed. The way Trent told it, he was overcome with emotion and got mad, mad enough to cause him to charge and attack Robbie. There's no doubt in my mind that Trent was the weaker of the two, but he was plenty strong and he must have caught Robbie off-guard. It wasn't planned or anything, and the police are calling it a crime of passion. They haven't arrested him yet. I asked them to wait until I had a chance to tell you myself. I couldn't bear the thought of you seeing it on the news."

"But Robert was his dad."

"Robbie didn't know that, and obviously Trent is off-balance. Who knows what he was thinking that night?"

Kayleigh needed to talk to someone, but she knew the only person who could comfort her was no longer here. She stood up, saying a quick good-bye before running to her car.

Later, at home, she cried. She cried for the senseless way her husband had died. She cried for all the years he had kept a secret from her, years she was sure he was in agony, and she cried for Trent. In some ways, she cried for him most of all.

She knew he was broken in so many ways. As much as it surprised even her, she knew she still wanted to reach out to him in love. She couldn't help but believe, if he were still alive, Robert would want to do the same thing.

*

Trent knew he was getting what he deserved. When the police had shown up at his apartment, he had opened the door and willingly let them take him away. He had been in his cell since then thinking about everything, his whole life really. He knew it would sound weird to anyone else, but other than missing Gracie, he liked it here. It certainly wasn't quiet, but he liked the noise. It kept him from being alone with his thoughts. He could choose when to pull them out and examine them, and then he could put them away and just listen to the voices around him. It was soothing in a way. For so long, thoughts of the night of the accident had tormented him, but he finally felt ready to deal with it all. It was ironic to him that he had spent his entire life wanting to belong to someone only to finally find a measure of peace when he was locked away where no one

cared about him at all.

Chapter Fifty-Five

Meghan had a little trouble following the directions Kayleigh had texted to her earlier, but she was glad they were moving past feeling the need to meet on neutral ground. She couldn't wait to hear this big idea her friend wanted to tell her. She knew she needed to share everything about Trent's phone call too, and she hoped she could talk Kayleigh into going to see him with her. She knew it was a stretch, but she couldn't get it out of her mind.

Kayleigh knew she was being ridiculous standing on the porch the way she was. Meghan wasn't supposed to be there for at least ten more minutes, but she couldn't stay inside and wait. She needed to hug her and tell her everything she knew. She needed somehow to sell her on the idea about taking care of Trent. She couldn't help but believe it wasn't too late for Meghan to finally be the mother he had always yearned for. It was certainly unconventional, but maybe somehow they could all find a way to become a family.

Frozen in Time

*

When the paper broke the story about the local firefighter who didn't die in a tragic accident like everyone had thought, Becca was grateful Kayleigh no longer had a subscription. She knew she would eventually see the words in print, but she hoped somehow to ease her into reading it. There was nothing written there that she didn't already know, but she still hoped to keep her friend from reliving that awful night all over again. Reading about it hurt her; she couldn't imagine how painful it would be for Kayleigh.

When Kayleigh had told her the plan she had made with Meghan, at first she had been worried. Going to the prison to visit the man who was accused of killing her husband didn't seem like a good idea to her, but once Kayleigh had told her about the dream and about how she was so sure Robert would want her to take care of his son, she hadn't been surprised by the first thing that had popped into her mind. When Romans 8:28 came to her again, she smiled, knowing this was God's way of using something terrible and letting good come from it.

She would never understand His ways, but she had finally learned she didn't have to.

*

Meghan and Kayleigh held hands as they waited for the prison guard to return with Trent. They had decided to tell him everything they had discussed. Both agreed that he needed to know that his life wasn't a mistake. They knew they had to convince him of that truth no matter how long it took.

Kayleigh couldn't keep it out of her mind how her husband would react if he knew he had a son. She could only imagine how years of thinking he had lost a baby had tortured him. She couldn't get one image out of her mind. For years she had watched her husband as he coached all kinds of young men, and she had always been in awe of how he seemed to connect with each and every one. She wondered, as she stood waiting to talk to the man who was so much a part of Robert, if he ever thought about his child while he was coaching. She liked to think that he did.

Feeling Meghan squeeze her hand, she knew she had been lost in her thoughts again. She smiled at her friend, letting her know that she was ready for everything that was about to happen. She could feel the way the hand that held her own trembled. Meghan barely looked old enough to have a child, much less one who was a grown man. Kayleigh had grown to love her like a sister, and even though everything in her wanted to offer comfort, she simple couldn't imagine what the other woman was feeling right now. She somehow knew simply being here was enough, so she smiled again before whispering, "He'll be here soon."

As soon as she saw Trent, Kayleigh was overcome with more love for him than she thought possible. She knew she should at least feel anger, maybe even rage, but all she felt was this incredible love. She clearly saw Robert in him now. She had the picture from her refrigerator with her. The prison guards had given her permission to keep it so she could share it with him. She knew she would know the right moment to give it to him. She could only hope when he looked at it, he would look past her image and see his dad in the background. She had prayed that it would bring him comfort. She knew better than to think she could do anything to erase all the pain he had lived with for so long, but she had decided to stick by his side from now on no matter what. She knew it was the one thing she could still do to show her husband how much she loved him.

*

Kayleigh was glad to be here with her two friends. She was happy to spend time with them today. Celebrating major days wasn't as hard for her as it had been when she had first lost Robert. She no longer dreaded their anniversary and both of their birthdays like she had at first, but today, on the anniversary she hated most of all, the day she had lost her husband, she was glad to have her friends with her.

Becca had gotten used to sharing her best friend with someone else. She was grateful Meghan had entered Kayleigh's life when she did. The two of them had been on such a journey together, and even though it still seemed strange to her that they both visited Trent so often, even that was starting to make sense.

So, as Kayleigh came back to the table carrying three large vanilla lattes, Becca had to smile. She knew today was a hard day for her, but she wasn't hiding in bed like she had so often that first year. She was truly moving on.

Kayleigh smiled as she looked at the two women who shared her table with her. She was grateful to have them both in her life. As they talked to each other, she leaned back and let her new favorite Bible verse flow through her mind. Yes, God had His hand on her. He had all along. She never could have imagined that this would be how her life would turn out. She always thought she would be a mom to a house full of children, but she had long ago given up that dream. After she realized it would only be her and Robert forever, she was able to look into their future and see them growing old together. In fact, she had been looking forward to it. Now, she was alone, but she was finally starting to understand that her life wasn't over. Even if all she ever got was the two friends sitting in front of her and the young man she had vowed to take care of the way she knew Robert would have, she was at peace.

It was true. God really did have a plan. And she was grateful to be a part of it.

Romans 8:28

"And we know that all things work together for good to them that love God, to them who are the called according to His purpose."

Sandy Brannan

Frozen in Time